FIC
MEY

Meyer, Susan,
1960-

Bla   FIC   hes.
       MEY

$19.99

Meyer, Susan,
1960-

Black radishes.

32007102009401

$19.99

DATE	BORROWER'S NAME	

Black Radishes

Black Radishes

SUSAN LYNN MEYER

DELACORTE PRESS

Text copyright © 2010 by Susan Lynn Meyer
Map © 2010 by Rick Britton

All rights reserved. Published in the United States by Delacorte Press,
an imprint of Random House Children's Books, a division of
Random House, Inc., New York.

Delacorte Press is a registered trademark and the colophon is a trademark of
Random House, Inc.

Visit us on the Web! www.randomhouse.com/kids
Educators and librarians, for a variety of teaching tools,
visit us at www.randomhouse.com/teachers

Library of Congress Cataloging-in-Publication Data
Meyer, Susan Lynn.
Black radishes / Susan Lynn Meyer. — 1st ed.
p. cm.
ISBN 978-0-385-73881-1 (hc : alk. paper)
ISBN 978-0-385-90748-4 (glb : alk. paper)
ISBN 978-0-375-89614-9 (e-book)
[1. Paris (France)—History—1940–1944—Fiction. 2. Holocaust, Jewish
(1939–1945)—Fiction. 3. Jews—France—Paris—Fiction. 4. Jewish
children—Fiction.] I. Title.
PS3613.E9793.B53 2010   813'.6—dc22   2009047613

The text of this book is set in 12.25-point Adobe Caslon.
Book design by Vikki Sheatsley
Printed in the United States of America
10 9 8 7 6 5 4 3 2 1
First Edition

For my father,
Jean-Pierre Meyer

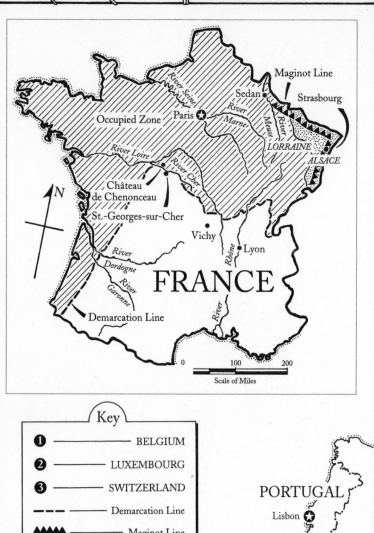

Maginot Line

Sedan

Strasbourg

Occupied Zone   Paris ★

River Seine

River

Marne

Meuse

River Rhine

LORRAINE

ALSACE

River Loire

River Cher

Château
de Chenonceau

St.-Georges-sur-Cher

Vichy •   Lyon •

Rhône

*River
Dordogne*

*River
Garonne*

River

FRANCE

Demarcation Line

N

0   100   200

Scale of Miles

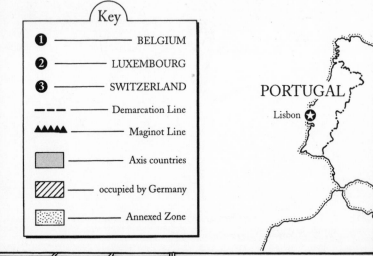

Key

❶ ———————— BELGIUM

❷ ———————— LUXEMBOURG

❸ ———————— SWITZERLAND

– – – – ———————— Demarcation Line

▲▲▲▲ ———————— Maginot Line

▨ ———————— Axis countries

▨ ———————— occupied by Germany

▨ ———————— Annexed Zone

PORTUGAL

Lisbon ★

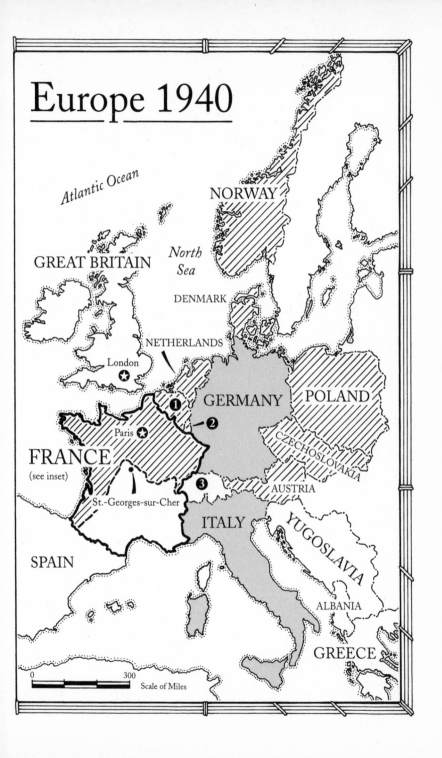

Europe 1940

Atlantic Ocean

NORWAY

GREAT BRITAIN

North
Sea

DENMARK

NETHERLANDS

London ✪

① GERMANY POLAND

Paris ✪ ②

CZECHOSLOVAKIA

FRANCE
(see inset)

③ AUSTRIA

St.-Georges-sur-Cher ITALY YUGOSLAVIA

SPAIN

ALBANIA

GREECE

0   300   Scale of Miles

1

Paris, March 1940

The Eiffel Tower was ugly. That was the only word for it, Gustave thought, gazing upward. It used to soar, a vivid red-brown, up into the sky over Paris. But now, quickly coated in dirty gray camouflage paint to disguise it from Nazi bombers, it somehow looked squat and sinister. From farther away in the city, earlier on this cool March afternoon, it had been hardly visible, melting eerily into the iron gray of the sky.

But that was the point, of course. And it was still obviously the Eiffel Tower. So why did the strange old man blocking Gustave's way on the sidewalk keep saying that it wasn't?

"That can't be the Eiffel Tower," the old man insisted again. "That's some gigantic piece of machinery."

"No, really, it is the Eiffel Tower," Gustave tried to explain hurriedly.

How could the old man not know about the camouflage paint? He was definitely French, and everybody in France knew about the war preparations. Was he senile?

"It's just that they painted it in case there is a bombing. You know, that's why they piled the sandbags up around all the monuments," Gustave told him.

The old man looked vaguely familiar. But Gustave was in too much of a hurry to find out why.

"Excuse me, but I need to go," he blurted out. "My Boy Scout troop is having a scavenger hunt. My team is the Eagles, and it's a race—"

But the old man interrupted.

"It's all nonsense, this war," he said. "The Nazis will never bomb Paris. We have the strongest army in Europe. But now, young man, can you tell me how to get to the post office?"

Gustave grimaced, dropped his rucksack, and started to explain. The old man had already insisted that Gustave stop to tell him about all the landmarks of Paris, and now he needed directions?

"So I turn right after three blocks?" asked the old man, after Gustave had patiently gone through the directions three times.

Gustave sighed. "No, left." Why did the man keep misunderstanding the directions or forgetting them, making Gustave repeat himself over and over? How were the Eagles ever going to win the scavenger hunt? But maybe it was hard for old people to remember things.

Gustave took a deep breath, and as he started going through the directions for the fourth time, a smile broke across the old man's face.

"Thank you, Boy Scout," he said. "You have been very helpful."

The old man turned and walked away, more briskly than Gustave would have thought possible. Gustave sighed in relief, grabbed his rucksack, and ran down the street.

His bag thumped against his back as he ran, but luckily it was light, so it didn't slow him down. His best friend, Marcel, had the bag with the scavenger-hunt treasures their team had collected. Most of the objects hadn't taken the three of them very long to find. A pocketknife, a teacher's signature, two green marbles, a safety pin, a math textbook, a canceled postage stamp, a gas mask, and a domino with nine dots. But a yellow feather? That was the item that all the teams were having trouble with. Of course, maybe one of the other Eagles, Marcel or Gustave's cousin Jean-Paul, had found one by now.

They had split up to look for the feather in order to triple their chances. Jean-Paul had raced home to pull feathers out of the pillow on his bed to see if one of them was yellow. That didn't seem very likely to work, but Jean-Paul had thought it was worth trying. Marcel was sure that his aunt had a hat with a yellow feather in it, so he had run off to her apartment to try to coax her into lending it for the afternoon. But it was very possible that she wouldn't want to let him borrow anything of hers. Last week, when Gustave and Jean-Paul had decided to go to the park to sail their boats in the fountain, Marcel, who didn't have a boat, had talked his aunt into lending him her umbrella—because it might rain, as he told her with a solemn face. The umbrella made a terrific boat, spinning around upside down in the water—but Marcel's aunt had been angry at him ever since because two of the spokes of the umbrella had broken. It worked fine if you held it right, but she was mad anyway.

Since the old man had delayed Gustave so long, both Marcel and Jean-Paul were probably already on their way back to the synagogue basement where the troop met, Gustave calculated. But there was no way of knowing whether either one of them had gotten the feather. So Gustave raced toward Monsieur Jouvet's hat shop, dodging around people on the sidewalk.

Monsieur Jouvet, who was an old friend of Papa's, would definitely have feathers, Gustave thought as he ran down the crowded street. Monsieur Jouvet was a round-faced, cheerful man who always offered Gustave candy from a jar he kept behind the counter. Once, he had given Gustave a tour of the back of the shop. He had ribbons and flowers and feathers there in all sorts of colors. If he had a yellow feather, surely he would let Gustave have it. But it was getting late. Was there enough time to run to the hat shop, get the feather, race back to the bus stop, catch a bus, and be back at the synagogue basement in time for the end of the scavenger hunt?

"Hey, Gustave!" Four boys from the Boy Scout troop burst out of a doorway in front of him. "Looking for one of these?" Pierre reached into his bag and waved a long, yellow feather in the air. "I bet we're the only ones who have one! Go, Bears!"

Gustave jumped and snatched at the feather, but Pierre held it out of his reach. "Where'd you get that?" Gustave panted.

"Pulled it out of my little brother's Indian headdress! Better hurry! The Bears are about to win!" The boys headed down the street, laughing and yelling.

Pierre's team acted as if they had everything. But maybe they didn't have a teacher's signature yet, Gustave thought hopefully. That one wasn't so easy either. And the Eagles had everything else, just the feather to go. Gustave sprinted down the last two blocks and around the corner.

He came to an abrupt stop where the display window of the hat shop should have been. Something was wrong. The iron shutters were pulled down over the shop front. A small handmade sign on the wall beside the iron shutters read CLOSED. SHOP OWNER MOBILIZED.

"Oh, no! Not him too!" Gustave gasped, thumping his fist against the sign in frustration. He leaned forward, his hands on his knees, catching his breath. So, Monsieur Jouvet was a soldier now too and away in the war, just like Jean-Paul's father and Marcel's, all of them off defending France against the Germans. Gustave would miss Monsieur Jouvet's smile and his silly jokes—not to mention the free candy.

Papa hadn't been mobilized with the other men his age because he walked with a limp from having had polio as a child. Last September, after the other men had left, Papa had stormed around the apartment for weeks, mad at everybody. Gustave twisted the ends of his Boy Scout neckerchief around his finger until it hurt, then let it go. He would never tell anyone this, especially not Marcel or Jean-Paul, but secretly he was glad that his father was still home.

Gustave turned and headed back toward the bus stop, wondering if he should try going to the Ménagerie, the zoo at the Jardin des Plantes. Maybe at the Ménagerie he could find a yellow feather that had fallen off some exotic bird. Was there time? He looked at his watch, a gift for his eleventh birthday in February. Four-forty—no time to try anywhere else. The scavenger hunt was over at five o'clock.

He was near the carousel at the Champ de Mars now. Usually it was busy with children, but now it was silent and deserted. Its paint had not been renewed that year. With their colors faded, the horses looked wild and unfamiliar, rolling their eyes and baring their teeth. Gustave suddenly wanted to be back in the synagogue basement with Marcel and Jean-Paul and the others. A few blocks away, a bus was approaching. He ran toward it, the wind whipping his hair into his eyes, and jumped on.

As he found a seat, Gustave remembered something. There wouldn't have been much point in going to the Ménagerie after all. The animals had all been evacuated to somewhere in the countryside to protect them in case of a bombing. Gustave imagined a parrot squawking while an air-raid siren sounded, dropping a yellow feather in its panic. If he had been a parrot, he would have lost a feather or two the first time that happened. Maybe every time it happened, to be perfectly honest.

All the air-raid signals so far had turned out to be false alarms. But he always woke up stunned, his heart thudding in his chest, when the alarms wailed through the darkness.

Those nights were all blurred together except for the first one, which was permanently etched in his memory. Papa's hand gripping his shoulder, heavy and hot. White searchlights flashing across the sky. The crowd of people jostling one another, hurrying down the steps. The dank smell of the underground shelter.

But all the parrots and other exotic birds and animals were safely hidden away now, far from Paris. So probably there wouldn't be any yellow feathers on the ground at the Ménagerie. Still, Gustave could have gone and checked if only the old man hadn't slowed him down so much.

Pierre was so annoying, Gustave thought, breathing on the cold window of the bus and tracing a design on it with his fingernail. Pierre always won everything. The winning team was going to get chocolate bars, plus ten points toward their team total for the year. Gustave looked at his watch again and then out the window, watching clouds race across the darkening sky. Did Marcel and Jean-Paul have a yellow feather? Or was Pierre's team going to win—*again*?

2

It was two minutes after five when Gustave pushed open the door to the room where the Boy Scouts were meeting. Monsieur Levi, the Scout leader, had already begun talking. He stopped as Gustave came in.

"Just in time, Gustave!" he said, smiling broadly. "If you have anything to add to your team's bag, you can bring it up."

"No, I don't have anything," said Gustave.

"No yellow feather for the Eagles?" Pierre jeered, putting his fingers at the corners of his mouth and pulling them down. "Aw, too bad!"

Gustave made a face at Pierre and squeezed in next to Marcel and Jean-Paul, who were sitting cross-legged on the floor.

"Hey!" whispered Jean-Paul, shifting over to make room for him. "So, no luck at the hat shop?"

"No—nothing in your pillow either?" Gustave whispered back. "And what about Marcel's aunt?"

Marcel leaned forward on the other side of Jean-Paul. "I remembered wrong. Her hat had a green feather." He grinned. "She said, 'Do you think I would have let you borrow it anyway, after what you did to my umbrella?' But I think she would have."

Monsieur Levi was talking up at the front. "So," he announced, "it would appear that the Bears have won. They completed the list and got back first." Pierre jumped to his feet, and he and the other three Bears whooped and cheered.

Marcel groaned. "Not again!"

"I said that it would *appear* that the Bears have won," Monsieur Levi said as the noise died down. "However"—he paused dramatically—"a secret test was part of the scavenger hunt."

The Boy Scouts were all giving him their full attention now. Monsieur Levi looked amused. "I asked your relatives to be out on the streets and to ask any boy in a Scout uniform for directions. Any Boy Scout who was not helpful got his team disqualified." Monsieur Levi grinned at the Bears. "Do you remember someone asking you for directions?"

"Oh, but that's not fair!" Pierre groaned, then laughed. "It was my own uncle! He kept not understanding what we told him, but I was sure that he knew his way around Paris!"

"He reports that you said, and I quote, 'What's the matter with you, Uncle? Have you become a complete idiot?' True?"

Pierre nodded sheepishly, and the Scouts broke into noisy laughter. Monsieur Levi held up his hand to quiet them. "So the second team to come back with all the items on the list, the Cougars, wins the scavenger hunt. They get the three chocolate bars, plus ten points for their team's total for the year."

The Cougars cheered.

"And"—Monsieur Levi held up his hand again—"I also award ten points to Gustave's team, the Eagles, because Antoine's grandfather, who was out on the street stopping Boy Scouts, reports that Gustave was 'supremely polite' to him for over fifteen minutes! I don't have any chocolate bars for the Eagles, but those ten points make the Eagles and the Bears tied for first place in the team totals for the year."

Jean-Paul whooped. "Tied for first! Go, Eagles!"

Marcel punched Gustave in the arm, grinning. "Supreme politeness! Where did that come from?"

Gustave looked at his friends in amazement. "Oh, I thought that man looked familiar. He's the reason I was so late—I think he slowed me down by about half an hour!"

As the Cougars went up to get their chocolate bars, Monsieur Levi went on. "So, boys, remember: Boy Scouts are helpful to all those in need. And, speaking of being helpful, I will be asking for volunteers in the coming weeks to help war refugees at the train stations. These families are fleeing their countries to come to France for safety. Often they don't speak French and don't know where to go. The boy who does the best job of helping the refugees will earn twenty points for his team total."

The Boy Scouts were already getting up and gathering their treasure-hunt bags and rucksacks. "Remember to return everything you borrowed for the scavenger hunt, boys," Monsieur Levi called. "See you next week!"

When Gustave and his friends were out on the sidewalk, Marcel reached into the bag and handed Jean-Paul the gas mask and Gustave the textbook, the domino, and the marbles. Jean-Paul slung the gas mask over his shoulder, and they started toward home.

"Bravo, Gustave!" said Jean-Paul. "Great job! But too bad we only got points for the end-of-the-year awards, not chocolate bars for right now. I'm starving!"

Gustave and Marcel laughed. "You're always starving!" said Gustave. "I can't believe we're tied for first. Now we just have to figure out how to beat the Bears before summer."

The wind was cold as they walked home. When they were a few blocks away from their neighborhood, Jean-Paul stopped to look into the window of a *boulangerie*. The smell of freshly baked bread made Gustave's stomach growl. But he still felt light and happy. What did it matter about being cold or hungry when he had just won ten points for the Eagles?

"Does anyone have any money?" Jean-Paul asked. "We could share something."

Gustave shook his head. "I haven't gotten any pocket money in a long time."

"Me either," said Marcel.

The door jingled, and a woman with a tiny dog on a leash stepped out of the bakery. Two long loaves of bread stuck out of her basket. The dog yipped and pulled toward Gustave. It was small, but its teeth looked sharp. Gustave moved aside to let them pass. A big man in a brown overcoat squeezed by the boys on the sidewalk and entered the *boulangerie,* where there was already quite a line of people waiting.

Marcel leaned toward the others. "Looking-up game!" he whispered.

Jean-Paul nodded, already putting on his serious face. Gustave laughed. It was a perfect place for the game, with so many people coming in and out of the bakery. The three of them looked up at the sky. Behind them, the door jingled again, and two men stepped out with long loaves of bread under their arms. Seeing that the boys were looking upward, the men paused and looked up too. A woman came out with her bread poking out of a string bag, holding the hand of a little blond girl who was tugging at her and fussing. She hushed the girl sharply and tilted her head back, peering up at the sky. A moment later, another woman, pulling a metal shopping cart, started to go around the two men, and then she too stopped and gazed upward.

Gustave felt warm bubbles of laughter rising up inside him. It was working so fast this time! He and Marcel and Jean-Paul used to play the looking-up game a lot when they were younger, but they hadn't done it in several years. Marcel had discovered the game by accident. It turned out that if all three of them stopped and looked up at the sky, outside an entrance to the Métro or in another busy spot in the city, other people would quickly stop and look up too.

Gustave glanced over his shoulder. More and more people were gathering behind them, completely blocking the sidewalk. Gustave smiled to himself and looked back up at the sky, which was turning an eerie pinkish gray. Mountainous storm clouds piled up in the east.

"Is it an airplane?" a woman whispered to one of the two men who had stopped first, her voice anxious.

"There's something behind that cloud," one of the men said. "Those boys saw it first."

"An airplane? French or German?" asked someone else. "Where?"

Gustave's stomach lurched. They thought that he and his friends had seen a German bomber? So that was why so many people had stopped so quickly. Should he explain to them that it was just a game? Gustave tapped Marcel's shoulder. Marcel looked back, saw all the people, and grinned, nudging Jean-Paul.

"But there's no air-raid signal," the woman with the little girl was saying in a petulant voice. Jean-Paul looked over at her blankly and then exploded into laughter. Marcel was laughing now too. The three of them slipped through the gathering crowd, trying to escape. Someone moved backward and stepped on Gustave's shoe, smashing his toes. He yanked his foot out from underneath, sweating. Someone else's elbow poked him in the back. Bodies were on all sides of him, crowding him in. Gustave's breath caught in his throat. He ducked down to slip underneath someone's arm and wiggled through the space along the bakery wall, scraping his shoulder against the rough bricks, and squeezed out past the edge of the crowd.

"Boys!" said one of the women, in disgust. "Just a trick to scare people."

"Boy Scouts too!" said another. "Shameful."

But they hadn't meant to scare anyone, Gustave thought indignantly. They hadn't been thinking about airplanes or bombs, just about how funny people look peering up at the sky. And they *had* looked funny. Should he explain? He paused.

A woman clutching an umbrella glared at Gustave. "Those aren't regular Boy Scouts. Look at their uniforms," she said, pointing. "See that badge? Those are *Éclaireurs Israélites*, Jewish Boy Scouts." She spat onto the sidewalk right next to Gustave, splattering his bare left leg. "They're Jews," she said. "Dirty Jews."

Gustave stared back at the woman's hostile eyes, unable to move to get away. So they were Jewish Boy Scouts. So what? There were Catholic Boy Scout troops, Protestant ones, and Jewish ones. All of them were Boy Scouts. Without thinking about what he was doing, he picked up his right foot and rubbed his sock against the repulsive wetness on the other leg to clean it. A drop of rain landed on his forehead and another on his cheek. Overhead, with an enormous crash of thunder, the storm broke.

Marcel darted back and pulled on Gustave's sweater. "Come on!"

Rain poured down. The glaring woman snapped open an umbrella and stomped off as the crowd scattered. Gustave ran with his friends toward home. Jean-Paul was still laughing, and Marcel carelessly glanced over his shoulder, whipping his wet hair away from his face.

"She's just some old crank," he yelled to Gustave. "Don't worry about it."

Gustave nodded. But as he remembered the worried faces, his stomach felt queasy. He hadn't scared the people on purpose, and neither had the others. Why was that woman so nasty? The looking-up game didn't have anything to do with being Jewish.

Gustave's shoelace was flopping. He stopped to tie it, pushing his dark hair out of his eyes. Marcel and Jean-Paul sprinted away from him through the downpour, yelling, but to Gustave, the water felt good, soaking into his shorts and his sweater, splashing down his legs, washing away the slimy spit. He started running again. The others were ahead of him, and he watched from behind as his friends turned into the narrow street where they all lived. When he caught up to them, first Jean-Paul and then Marcel leapt over a huge puddle of water, splashing down on the other side. Water always accumulated there when it rained.

As Marcel and Jean-Paul disappeared into their apartment buildings, calling back to him through the rain, Gustave stopped, his heart still thudding, and looked down to see if the drain at the curb was clogged again. Large words were scrawled across the street in white paint, partly covered by the puddle. The writing, all in capital letters, wavered under the water, but one word stood out. *"JUIFS." Jews.*

Gustave leaned over to see what the other words were. As he read them, his wet clothes suddenly grew cold against his skin. It felt as if an angry voice were shouting at him and at the other people in his neighborhood. At the men and women living nearby, who were just now doing their shopping, coming home, starting dinner in their kitchens, hanging up their hats, opening the newspaper. At all the small children in the apartments along the street, who were playing with toy cars on the floor, poking their brothers and sisters, sucking their thumbs, asking when dinner would be ready. At older girls, who were trying out new dance steps to the music on the radio, rinsing vegetables in kitchen sinks, or reading, stomach down on their beds. And at all the boys Gustave's age, who were just now dashing home through the rain from the synagogue, shouting goodbye to one another, and swinging their bags of scavenger-hunt treasures.

"LA FRANCE AUX FRANÇAIS!" the words on the street read. *"JUIFS HORS DE FRANCE!" France for the French! Jews out of France!*

3

By the time Gustave had reached the second floor of his apartment building, he had decided not to tell his parents about the woman who had spat at him or about the words on the street. Maman got upset too much of the time lately as it was. But he wanted to get to the bathroom right away to wash his leg with soap. He pushed open the apartment door and immediately got a whiff of Aunt Geraldine's flowery perfume. Her coat was hanging on the peg next to Papa's, and he heard voices coming from the living room.

If Gustave said hello politely to Jean-Paul's mother, the way he was supposed to, it would slow him down in getting to the bathroom. His leg felt contaminated, as if it wouldn't be part of him again until it was washed. Maybe he could slip by without being noticed. Gustave left his muddy shoes by the door and tiptoed into the hall, his socks making wet footprints on the wooden floor. But he stopped when he heard raised voices.

"We can't go," Aunt Geraldine wailed. "We can't just leave. How will my husband find us when he comes back from the war?"

Gustave peered into the room. Aunt Geraldine was perched on the sofa with her legs crossed. Maman sat forward in an armchair, and Papa paced, frowning, in front of the windows.

"But we applied together for the immigration visas for both families!" Maman gestured wearily, as if she had said the same thing many times before. "David wants you to go to America. He wants you to be safe!"

"But we were all going to go to America together!" Aunt Geraldine moaned. "The children and I can't leave without him. No!" She waved her hands in front of her face as if she were brushing something away. "The war should be over in a few months, when the Nazis realize they can't do anything to France."

"But it is dangerous right now," Maman insisted. "*Because* of the war. We can't wait. You really *must* come with us."

Aunt Geraldine adjusted her skirt. "You worry too much. When David comes home, he and I will talk about whether we should emigrate. But the American consul said that we might not get the immigration visas or that it might take a long time. Meanwhile, the children and I will stay here in Paris, like civilized people, not go running off into the countryside." Aunt Geraldine smoothed her skirt's silken folds.

Maman leaned back and sighed in frustration. The floor creaked under Gustave's feet, and they all looked up and saw him.

"Oh, the boys are back," said Aunt Geraldine, sniffing. "I have to go." She got up, quickly embraced Maman, Papa, and then Gustave, kissing each of them on both cheeks, and ran out of the room. Maman hurried after her.

What were they talking about? Going to America? Leaving France? Gustave remembered the graffiti—"France for the French! Jews out of France!"—and his stomach hurt. But his family *was* French. Weren't they? Papa had grown up in Switzerland, but he had lived in France since he had been a young man. Maman and her sister, Aunt Geraldine, had both been born in France, and so had Maman's parents and her grandparents. The hospital where Gustave had been born was right here in Paris. Of course they were French. French *and* Jewish.

Maman came back into the room, rubbing her arms as if she felt cold. She looked right at Gustave, but she didn't seem to notice his wet clothes.

"What's the matter?" Gustave asked. "Why were you and Aunt Geraldine arguing?"

"Let's sit down," Maman said. "We have to talk."

Something was definitely wrong. Maman usually made a big fuss about his changing immediately out of wet clothes—especially before sitting on the upholstered furniture. Gustave perched on the edge of the sofa. His dirty leg felt awkward, and he stuck it out in front of him. He picked up the embroidered pillow next to him and put it on his lap, scratching at the beads.

"What?" he said hoarsely when nobody said anything.

"We're going to leave Paris," said Papa finally.

Gustave stared at him. They really were leaving, then.

"But why?" he cried. Maybe Papa or Maman had seen the writing too.

"We want to get as far away as we can from Nazi Germany," Maman answered. "It will be safer. The Nazis treat Jews very badly."

Safer from the Nazis? Gustave's thoughts swirled, confused. But that writing wasn't in German; it was in French. And with the French defense so strong, how could the Nazis get into France?

Papa sat down on the sofa next to Gustave. He added gently, "You remember how we talked about what's been happening in Poland and why it's such a good thing that Marcel's parents moved away from there just before he was born?"

Gustave shuddered, remembering that day when he had gone to the movies with Jean-Paul to see *Robin Hood*. He and Jean-Paul had saved their pocket money and waited a long time to see the film, but Gustave hardly remembered it—because before *Robin Hood* began there had been a newsreel. During the movie, the images from the newsreel repeated over and over again in his head, blocking out the story on the screen. Instead of watching Robin Hood and his Merry Men, he kept seeing the Nazis driving their tanks into Poland and forcing people into camps. That night, Gustave had shouted in his sleep, and Papa had come in, bleary-eyed, in his bathrobe, to talk with him. But there hadn't been much that he could say to make Gustave feel better except that it was all far away.

Gustave had dreamt about that newsreel for weeks afterward. The Nazis shot people in Poland just because they felt like it, just to show that they were in charge. They especially hated Jews. They put them and other people they didn't like in places surrounded by barbed wire, places called internment camps. A few refugees had escaped to Belgium and France and had told people about it. The camps were like prisons. There were soldiers with guns. They gave the people in the camp almost no food, and the living quarters were crowded and filthy. People died there from the cold, from hunger and diseases. They treated the people in the camps "worse than animals," the narrator had stated in his deep, sonorous voice. "But France and civilization will defeat barbarism!" he had proclaimed. "The French army is strong!"

"But the French army is strong," said Gustave. "That could never happen here?" It came out sounding more like a question than he had meant it to.

"France *is* strong," Papa agreed. "But you know how your mother worries." He smiled at Maman. "She has convinced me that we would be safer if we left Paris. We have applied for visas to go to America with Jean-Paul's family, but that process takes a long time."

"Leave France?" It seemed impossible to imagine.

"Maybe we will," Papa said. "We'd be lucky if we could get permission to immigrate to the United States. I'm hopeful, because I have a cousin there. That helps. But it still isn't certain. We'll see. For now, we are going to go live in a small French village."

"With a madman like Hitler in charge of Germany, invading one country after another, it's better to be in an out-of-the-way place," Maman explained. She patted Gustave's knee, but he could tell that she was talking to Papa as much as to him.

Papa nodded slowly. "Who knows what the future holds here for the Jews? More and more French people seem to hate us, just like Hitler and the Nazis. I hope that you haven't encountered any of that, Gustave, but these days it is everywhere."

Papa looked at Gustave searchingly. Gustave swallowed and looked down.

"I have rented us a place to stay in the countryside, in a nice little village near a river," Papa went on. "You'll like it, I'm sure."

Well, at least they would be in France, not in a whole different country where he couldn't even speak the language. America was too far away even to think about. But how could they leave their life in Paris?

"But what about school?" Gustave asked. "What about the end-of-year prizes? I think I'm going to win the history prize again this year! Maybe math too. Aren't we going to wait until school is over? And what about the store?"

"Papa has been trying for months to find someone to take over the lease for the store," Maman said. "Now that he has found someone, we are going to leave. Being safe is the most important thing."

Gustave couldn't believe it. His parents never thought

22

that anything was more important than school. Maman still kept the history prize he had won two years ago, a book inscribed on the front leaf by his teacher, in a place of honor in the bookcase with glass doors in the dining room. Sometimes she even took it out to show visitors who stayed for dinner. And now, when he was almost sure to win another prize, she wanted to leave Paris?

And Papa loved his store. He had opened it when Gustave was just a little boy. Gustave had visited his father there ever since he could remember. The shop had its own special smell, like chalk and cloth and new shoe leather, mixed with the floor-cleaning soap Papa used. How could Papa give it all up?

"What is it called, the village where we are going?" Gustave asked. He heard his voice quaver and bit down, hard, on his lip.

"Saint-Georges," Maman said. "It's in the Loire Valley. Do you remember it? We went there once for vacation with Jean-Paul's family when you were younger."

"No," said Gustave, pressing his finger down over the bumpy beads embroidered on the pillow. He ran his finger over and over the beaded outline of a leaf. One bead was missing, and it bothered him every time he jumped his finger over the space.

"We're leaving on Friday," Papa added.

"On Friday!" Gustave shoved the pillow aside, and it fell off the sofa. "But I *can't* go now. The Eagles just tied with the Bears today for first place at Boy Scouts. We have to beat them! Can't we just wait until July, when the team prizes are awarded?"

Maman's face tightened. "We can't wait any longer," she said. "It's too dangerous. We have to go now."

Gustave stood up and looked dazedly at his parents.

"But we're all going together, right?" he said. A bad feeling started to come over him. "You'll convince Jean-Paul's family to come too? And what about Marcel and his mother?"

Maman sighed. "I tried to tell Madame Landau that she and Marcel should get out of Paris," she said. "She says she can't afford to live if she leaves her job."

"What about Aunt Geraldine and Jean-Paul and the baby?" Gustave insisted.

Maman shook her head. Gustave was startled to notice that she had tears in her eyes—Maman, who never cried. "No," she said. "I've been begging Geraldine and begging her. How can I leave my little sister and her children behind? But she says no. She says she won't come with us."

Gustave washed his leg off in the bathroom, scrubbing his shin with a soapy washcloth until it stung. Then he stood in his room, staring at the map that he had pinned up on the wall a few years ago, when they first started studying geography in school. The countries of Europe were outlined in black ink on the white paper. He could use the map to keep track of the war.

Somewhere in his desk were his watercolors. Gustave found them in the back of a drawer. He filled a little cup with water from the bathroom and carried it back to his room, walking slowly so as not to spill it. He put it down on the bookshelf and opened the paints. France and Britain were allied against Germany. He carefully outlined France and England in blue, his favorite color, and painted them in. When he dipped the brush to clean it, blue paint swirled into the water. He would use red for Nazi Germany, since red was one of the colors on the Nazi flag. Gustave covered Germany in red paint.

But Germany was expanding and expanding. In the last two years, Germany had taken over Austria and Czechoslovakia. Gustave wet the brush again and painted Austria and Czechoslovakia red. And then in September, Germany had invaded Poland. That's when France and Britain had declared war. Gustave quickly washed red paint over Poland, trying not to think about what might have happened to Marcel's family if they had still been living there.

A drip of red paint ran down the map, and Gustave used his handkerchief to clean it off. All that red made Europe look as if it had some horrible, contagious disease. And the disease pressed right up against the French border.

But Antoine's grandfather had said that France had the strongest army in Europe. And everyone talked so proudly about the Maginot Line, the underground forts France had built all along the German border, along the border between France and Luxembourg, and a little way along the line between France and Belgium. Gustave had seen newspaper photographs of them.

Thinking about the huge guns pointing up from underground toward Germany made him feel better. He grabbed his fountain pen out of his desk drawer and drew in the

Maginot Line, running the pen up and down, from the northern end of Switzerland, all along Germany, up to the southern end of Belgium, and back again, until he had made a thick, dark border.

Gustave sat down on his bed and looked across the room at the map. With the Maginot Line inked in, it looked much better.

"The *Boches* will never get past that," he said out loud, using the insulting French word for Germans. "Just let them try." Terrible things were happening in other countries. But the Nazis would never control France.

4

At school the next day, Gustave's teachers didn't seem surprised when he told them he was leaving. Lately, more and more people had been emptying out of Paris. In fact, Gustave realized, looking around the room, almost a third of the desks were vacant, the desks of all the kids who had left since September. But when they heard the news, Jean-Paul and Marcel stared at Gustave in dismay.

"Why do you have to go?" Jean-Paul groaned after school. "We were going to have a marbles tournament, re-member? And you're going to miss the end-of-the-year camping trip, and summer, and . . . everything."

"I know," said Gustave. He looked down at his feet. Why did Jean-Paul have to remind him?

"Yeah, and what if there's another politeness test at Boy Scouts?" Marcel said, poking Gustave in the shoulder until he looked up again. "Jean-Paul and I will get negative points! But seriously, Gustave, when are you coming back?"

"Nobody said when. After the war, I guess."

"Hey, since we're cousins, maybe your parents would let you stay with us, Gustave," Jean-Paul suggested, his face brightening. "Then you wouldn't have to go."

Gustave's heart leapt. "Yeah, maybe!" he said excitedly. "I'll ask."

But as Gustave got closer to home, he walked slowly, feeling less hopeful. Maman might get angry if he told her what Jean-Paul had said. She got angry a lot lately. But if he didn't ask, there would be no chance at all. Gustave grasped the doorknob tightly, feeling the coolness of the metal under his damp hand, and pushed open the apartment door. Packing paper was everywhere, and coats and suits were draped over the sofa and chairs. The portraits of Great-grandmother and Great-grandfather had been taken down, and the spaces on the wall where they had been looked strangely blank. Maman was standing in the middle of the living room. There was dust in her hair, and loose strands fell around her face.

"Oh, Gustave," she said. "Good, you're back. I need you to pack up your things. There's a suitcase in your room."

Gustave's pulse raced. It was now or never. "Why can't I just stay in Paris?" he demanded. "Jean-Paul says I can live with them."

"Absolutely not," Maman answered, frowning. "Papa and I have already explained this to you, Gustave. We are moving to the country. All of us, together."

Gustave shoved his hands into his pockets, feeling his

fingers tremble. "Aunt Geraldine said you worry too much," he burst out. "I heard her."

Maman pinched her lips together. "We are going, Gustave," she said evenly, "and you are going too. Now, pack."

In his room, Gustave kicked at the leg of his bed. Why did grown-ups get to decide everything? He stared miserably at the suitcase Maman had left open on his bed. Papa sometimes took that little suitcase when he went away on business for two or three days. How was Gustave supposed to fit everything inside? He didn't want to leave anything important behind. He started piling all his toys and books onto the bed and into the open suitcase.

Half an hour later, Maman put her head in the door. "How are you doing with the packing?" she asked.

Gustave stepped back, scowling, and pointed at the already-overloaded suitcase on the bed.

"Oh, no, Gustave!" Maman said sharply. "Use your head! Not playthings! We can take very little with us. You need clothes, especially warm clothes."

Gustave looked back at her in disbelief. "You mean, all I can bring is clothes?"

His mother came in and sat down on the bed. "I have room in one box for two or three of your books and toys," she answered, more gently. "But there's only a little bit of space. The truck is going to be very full. I'm sorry, Gustave," she added. "But we all have to leave behind things we love."

After she left, Gustave sat on the bed for a long time. A damp cloud, dark and heavy, seemed to be pressing down on him. When he got up, he dumped his toys out onto his bed and looked slowly around his room. He had almost forgotten to pack the map on the wall, he realized. He took it down and folded it up carefully. He would need that and his paints to keep track of the war. He picked up his Boy Scout manual and his two favorite books, *The Three Musketeers* and *Around the World in Eighty Days,* and put them on the end of the bed, next to the paints and the map. That was already more than three things. But since it was mostly books, Maman would probably let him bring one more toy.

But how could he choose only one? Gustave picked up his new sailboat and ran a finger over its shiny blue and white paint. Uncle David had given him and Jean-Paul each a sailboat last summer to sail in the fountains in the parks. Saint-Georges was near a river, so a boat would be good to have. But then he saw Monkey, partly hidden under his train set on the bed, and his heart tightened. He had almost forgotten him. Monkey's head tilted slightly to one side. A gold post in his ear and the bright black, beady eyes looking out from his face gave him a mischievous air.

The small stuffed animal had belonged to Gustave ever since he had been a baby, and Monkey had often been a part of his games with Jean-Paul and Marcel. Gustave remembered the time a few years ago when, for weeks, the three of them had played shipwreck. Monkey had been a mascot left behind by pirates. Another time they had played spies. Monkey had been their most powerful secret weapon, trained to climb the outside of buildings, pry open windows, and break into safes. They didn't play with the little stuffed animal very much anymore. But having Monkey in Saint-Georges would be the next-best thing to having his friends there. Before he could change his mind, Gustave put Monkey on top of the books and the paint box and took the pile out to Maman.

After dinner, Marcel and Jean-Paul came over to help carry things down the stairs because Papa's bad leg made dealing with the stairs difficult.

Gustave thrust the sailboat at Marcel. "Do you want to borrow it?" he asked. "That way you won't get into any more trouble about umbrellas."

"Really? Wow!" Marcel held the sailboat reverently. "Thanks! I promise there won't be a scratch on it when you come back."

Marcel hurried home to put the sailboat away where it would be safe, and when he came pounding back up the stairs to Gustave's apartment, the three boys carried down the boxes and suitcases, an armchair that had belonged to Maman's great-grandmother, and the mattresses from the beds. When Papa opened the back of the delivery truck, Gustave saw why they could take only five boxes, plus the suitcases. The truck was already two-thirds full with rolls of cloth and boxes of shoes from the store.

"Why are you taking so much stock with you, Uncle Berthold?" Jean-Paul asked. "Are you going to open up a new store in Saint-Georges?"

Papa heaved the big mattress from his and Maman's bed until it stood upright, and wiped the sweat off his forehead. "Well, I don't know about a new store," he said. "I'm not sure if we'll be there long enough for that to make sense.

But I couldn't sell off all the stock, and it's too valuable not to bring along."

Marcel was the tallest, so he helped Papa push the mattresses onto the top of the truck and cover them with canvas, while Gustave and Jean-Paul tied them down with ropes. When everything was fitted into the back of the delivery truck, Papa pushed the door shut.

It latched with a final-sounding click. His family's whole life was in that truck now, Gustave thought. At least, the part of their life that they were able to take with them.

Papa reached out and pulled all three of the boys into a jostling embrace. "Be good, boys," he said hoarsely to Marcel and Jean-Paul. "Take care of your families." Then he went back into the building, leaving Gustave to say goodbye to his friends.

The three of them glanced at each other and looked down at the ground. Gustave couldn't think of anything to say. The quiet stretched out a long time, too long. Suddenly, Gustave remembered the way they used to play Three Musketeers. "All for one!" he cried, holding out his fist.

Marcel looked up, smiled, and put his hand on top of Gustave's fist. Jean-Paul clapped his hand on top of Marcel's. Gustave looked at their three hands there, clasped together. "All for one—one for all!" the three of them chanted at the same time. "Jean-Paul, Marcel, Gustave—together forever!"

"Jean-Paul!" Aunt Geraldine's voice sounded faintly from down the street.

"Bye!" Jean-Paul said quickly, and darted toward home.

Marcel and Gustave looked at each other for a long

moment. "So," Marcel said, "you'll come back as soon as we've knocked off the Boches?"

Gustave nodded. "We'll teach them not to mess with us," he said. But his throat felt tight. When would that be? When would he see Marcel and Jean-Paul again? Gustave stood and watched as Marcel ran home, across the street and along the sidewalk, through the gathering darkness.

5

Maman wanted to leave very early so that they could be all unpacked in Saint-Georges by nightfall. It had rained again overnight, and it was the darkest morning Gustave had ever seen. Outside, the city was strangely dim and quiet. As Gustave climbed into the truck, the edge of the sun came up, turning the creamy stones of the buildings a pale pink and glittering on the wet iron railings of the balconies. When Papa started the engine, a flock of pigeons rose up noisily from the apartment building opposite them, black against the pastel colors of the sky.

Gustave listened to the loud, flapping wings as they drove away in the truck, every moment getting farther away from home. It was so unfair, he thought. Why did he have to go, if Jean-Paul and Marcel were staying behind? The pigeons could fly wherever they wanted to. They didn't have to worry about war, about Germany, or about guns and bombs. They didn't have to worry about being Jewish either. He closed his eyes, the flapping wings still sounding in his ears, and fell asleep.

He woke up when they stopped to eat. As they drove on after lunch, Gustave watched the changing landscape outside the window. Farm fields stretched out on either side of the road. It was warmer than at home in Paris, and spring was further along. Trees were coming into leaf, and a green mist covered the fields. After a while the road began to wind through small villages, clusters of red-roofed houses with here and there a post office or a café. They crossed a bridge over a wide river and wound through more tiny villages. And then Gustave saw a sign: ST-GEORGES-SUR-CHER.

"Ah, it seems so peaceful here," Maman breathed. Gustave could hear the relief in her voice. But what was so great about it being peaceful? Compared with Paris, Saint-Georges looked empty and boring. The only person Gustave could see was an old man sweeping the sidewalk in front of a shop.

Papa turned and drove up a hill, following a narrow, winding road. He stopped at a white stone-and-stucco house. A narrow strip of garden and a low stone wall separated it from the road.

"Here it is!" Papa called out cheerfully. "The house is divided into two parts. We'll be renting the left-hand side. Madame Foncine is the landlady, and she lives in the other half. She wrote that the key will be between the roots of the potted tree next to the steps."

"What a beautiful house!" Maman said. "It looks as if it's about a century old."

The house had three levels, and one of them was an attic. Gustave had read about attics in books, but, living in a city, he had never been able to go into one. At least exploring the attic would be something interesting to do, he thought, although it would have been a lot more fun if Jean-Paul and Marcel were there to do it with him.

Still, Gustave wanted to explore it, and, after the long trip, he was really starting to need the bathroom. He ran ahead of his parents and found the key between the roots of the small tree in the planter, brushed the soil off it, and fit it into the lock.

The door squeaked open. Inside, it was dark and smelled musty. When Maman opened the windows and shutters, they saw a small room with large, heavy country furniture— a sofa, two armchairs, and a large oak armoire. A radio sat on a table in a dark corner. Stairs separated the living room from an old-fashioned kitchen with a large sink and a pump. Gustave ran up the squeaky steps to the second floor. It was musty up there too.

The smaller bedroom must be for him. He pulled open the windows, pushed out the shutters, and looked out over a walled garden behind the house. Two hazelnut trees grew there, one on each side of a small shed. Inside the room, a narrow bed stood against the wall beside an old night table. There was nothing else but a dusty chest of drawers holding a basin and pitcher for washing.

But how did you get up to the attic? Gustave pulled open a door in the wall of his room, feeling hopeful. Maybe he had his own private entrance and the attic could be his secret place. But it was just a closet. Maman and Papa's room didn't even have a closet, only an armoire. Gustave tapped the walls to see if they sounded hollow anywhere. They didn't. There was no pull-down trapdoor on the ceiling of either bedroom or in the hallway. And where was the bathroom, anyway? Gustave wondered. The situation was getting urgent.

Gustave ran to the landing halfway down the stairs. Maman was already dusting the living room, and Papa was bringing in boxes.

"Where's the bathroom?" he shouted. "I need it, and I can't find it!"

Papa grinned up at him. "Outside in the backyard! And there's a chamber pot under your bed for nighttime. Remember how Aunt Geraldine complained that the country was uncivilized? Now you know why. But you're a Boy Scout—you know how to rough it, right?"

Gustave ran to the shed in the backyard. So that was what it was. It smelled, but he needed it too badly to be fussy. When he came out, Papa was pulling the mattresses down from the top of the truck.

"How do you get up to the attic, Papa?" Gustave called.

"Come help me carry up the mattresses," answered Papa. "We can put them on the bed frames, and I'll help you look." But Papa couldn't find an entrance or a trapdoor either.

"But there *has* to be a way up to the attic," said Gustave. "Otherwise, what's the point of having one?"

"There must only be stairs up to it from the other side of the house," Papa told Gustave.

"Oh, why couldn't we rent the *other* side?" Gustave moaned.

Papa shrugged. *"Désolé, mon vieux,"* he said. *Sorry, old pal.* "That's where Madame Foncine lives."

"Why does *she* get the good side?" Gustave muttered under his breath. It was so unfair. The attic was the most interesting thing about the house, and Gustave couldn't get into it. He turned and pounded down the stairs.

"I'm going outside to explore!" he shouted, pushing open the front door.

"Unpack first," said Maman, sticking her head out of the kitchen.

"Do I have to? Can't I do it later?"

"Now," said Maman.

Maman had already opened the box with Gustave's things in it, so unpacking didn't take long. Gustave tucked Monkey into the loose pocket of his pants and put his books into the bottom of the armoire in the living room. He lugged his suitcase up the stairs and put his clothes into the bureau. When he pulled open the bottom drawer, he found some old jigsaw puzzles and an empty picture frame, but he didn't have enough clothes to need that drawer anyway, so he left them there. Maman handed Gustave a pile of bedding, and he made the bed, spreading his familiar blue blanket on top. He set the paints on the shelf under the night table and pinned the map of Europe up on the wall. When everything was unpacked in his bedroom, Gustave glanced around. It was starting to feel as if it belonged to him, but it still seemed empty. Then Gustave remembered Monkey, in his pocket. He pulled him out and sat him against the lamp on the night table. Now it looked more like home.

Maman caught Gustave again as he was heading outside. "While you're out, find the bakery and buy us two baguettes," she said, handing him some money. "We can use those instead of challah, since there's no time to make it this afternoon. Be back before sunset. Remember, it's Shabbat tonight."

Gustave walked up the road to the end, turned left, and wandered along another road that wound between closely clustered white and gray houses. The afternoon sun was warm on his shoulders. He was sure that if he kept walking, he would find some other boys. But road after road was deserted. Each was lined with stone walls and heavy iron gates. Behind the walls, the quiet gray stone-and-stucco houses, their windows sealed off with white wooden shutters, seemed to turn their backs to him, closing him out.

It was profoundly quiet. No traffic sounds, no voices. The cooing of doves, fluttering here and there around the roofs of the houses, resonated in the stillness. At the bottom of the hill, on the main street of the town, Gustave saw an old woman with a cane who was slowly starting up the hill and two younger women who stood talking to one another by the post office. But no kids. Was this a village with only grown-ups?

Gustave turned off the main street and wandered up another hill. He walked until the houses stopped and the farm fields began. Still no children anywhere. Gustave was starting to wish that he had taken Monkey along in his pocket for company. He turned and began wandering back to the center of the village to buy the bread. The empty road stretched out ahead of him, etched with sun and shadow.

What were Marcel and Jean-Paul doing now? Gustave felt a sharp twinge of loneliness. It was past four o'clock, so school was out. Maybe they were doing their homework together on Jean-Paul's kitchen table. Or maybe they had finished, and now they were kicking a soccer ball around in the park. In the middle of the road was a large white stone. Gustave kicked at it aimlessly, and it skidded ahead of him. The game would be to kick the stone so that it skidded over the sunny areas and came to a stop only in the areas of shadow, he decided. He was doing well until the stone got stuck in a dent in full sunshine.

"Interference," Gustave said out loud. "That doesn't count."

He picked up the stone and kicked it again, down the dusty road.

The house on the right had a high, dark, bumpy wall. Gustave wondered if the white stone would write on it. He tried, and the stone scraped loudly, leaving a faint trace. Suddenly, a hand pushed open a high black metal gate on the other side of the road, and a small boy's face peered out.

"Hi!" Gustave called. He ran toward the boy, waving.

"Come back here, Jean-Christophe!" a woman's voice scolded. The boy darted inside, letting the gate slam shut behind him. The sound rang through the stillness.

Gustave stared at the closed gate. Why wouldn't that boy's mother let him play? He was little, but at least he would have been someone to hang around with. Saint-Georges was so different from the cheerful, bustling streets of Paris. Didn't anyone live here? If Gustave had walked around his neighborhood at home for half an hour, he would have run into ten or fifteen boys ready to play. He kicked the stone again, too hard, and it bounced with a clang off a rusty green metal gate. Something huge and hairy lunged at the gate from the other side, barking and snarling. His heart thudding, Gustave grabbed the stone and darted away. It was an enormous Alsatian dog, penned in the yard. It leapt, growling and slavering, trying to get its muzzle over the top. Too late, Gustave noticed the hand-made sign: CHIEN MÉCHANT. *Mean Dog.* Many of the houses had that sign or ATTENTION: CHIENS DE GARDE. *Warning: Guard Dogs.* Even the animals were unfriendly here.

Gustave shoved the rock into his pocket and ran down the road. He didn't feel like exploring anymore. He would buy the bread and go back home.

At least there were people in the bakery. Three stout ladies stood in front of the counter, chatting with the woman behind it. Beside one of them stood a tall, thin boy around Gustave's age. As Gustave pushed open the door, they all turned to look at him and fell silent. After a moment, the women went back to their conversation. But the boy was still staring at Gustave. His hair was pale and his eyes were clear, almost colorless. The boy looked Gustave up and down, taking his time.

"Are you renting from Madame Foncine?" he asked after a few minutes. "You're those city people from Pa-ris?" He said the word "Paris" in a mocking way, as if there were something ridiculous about it.

"Yes," said Gustave.

The boy didn't respond.

Gustave fidgeted, rubbing the back of his neck. He couldn't think of anything to say. Obviously the boy lived here, so there was no point in asking that.

"Do you know Madame Foncine?" Gustave finally managed. The boy didn't nod or answer. He just stared silently at Gustave with those peculiar clear eyes. Gustave felt himself flushing hot with anger. Why was the boy acting so strange? When Gustave's turn came, he quickly asked for his two baguettes, paid, and went out the door, feeling the boy watching him the whole time.

It was a relief to be outside. Gustave started back along the main street, toward the new house, stopping to look at a small fountain shaded by short, gnarled trees. In the middle, the stone figure of a dolphin waved its tail upward, while water bubbled merrily out of its mouth. Gustave put his baguettes on the wall that surrounded the fountain and leaned over to look down into it. Under the wavering water, coins shimmered on the bottom.

"Hey, Paris kid!" a taunting voice called out. Gustave turned. The pale-eyed boy from the bakery ran at him and shoved him, hard, making him lose his balance on the fountain's edge. The water slammed against Gustave's head and back. He felt a shock of cold as he went under. The boy was peering over the wall of the fountain when Gustave came up, gasping.

"Go back where you came from!" he jeered. Then his face disappeared, and Gustave heard his feet running away.

Gustave scrabbled for a foothold on the slippery bottom of the fountain. Next to him, one of the baguettes bobbed in the water, slowly submerging. He climbed over the edge, weighed down by his wet clothes. The other baguette was teetering precariously on the edge of the fountain. He grabbed it and ran after the boy, water sloshing in his shoes.

"What did you do that for?" he shouted. But the boy had vanished between the buildings or maybe into one of them.

"Coward!" Gustave shouted again, but only his own voice echoed back at him. He looked around. The shadows were long on the bare road. He had no idea where the boy had gone, and Maman wanted him home before sundown. He checked the change in his pocket. Not enough money to buy a third baguette to replace the waterlogged one. Maman was going to be upset not to have the customary two loaves of bread for the Sabbath. Sloshing and shivering, Gustave slowly made his way back up the hill toward his new house.

"I did it," Maman was saying as Gustave opened the door. "I got us ready to have our first Shabbat in Saint-Georges."

She and Papa stood together by the table. While Gustave had been outside exploring, Maman had transformed the dark kitchen. Her copper-bottomed cooking pots shone warmly on the walls, and the open shutters let in the smells of spring, the soft cooing of the doves, and the glow of the late afternoon. The white tablecloth and polished silver candlesticks gleamed. Maman's face was calm and serene, ready to welcome in the Sabbath. But when she turned to look at Gustave, her expression changed.

"What happened?" she exclaimed. "How did you get so wet? Oh, your shoes too! And couldn't you buy a second baguette?"

"Sounds like an odd boy," said Papa when Gustave had finished reluctantly telling them about the boy from the bakery. "I guess he doesn't like strangers. Or maybe he resents city people."

"What did he call you, exactly?" asked Maman, twisting her fingers together. "He didn't say 'Jew,' did he?"

"No. Just 'Paris kid.' " Gustave's stomach felt hollow. "Don't they like Jews here either?"

"I don't imagine that many people in Saint-Georges know any Jews," said Papa. "It's a small Catholic village. The families here have lived in this area for generations. Don't worry about it, Lili," he said to Maman. "If we only have one loaf of bread, that's what we'll use. Go change quickly, Gustave, and then let's welcome in Shabbat."

When Gustave came down in dry clothes, Maman pulled her lace shawl over her head and struck a match to light the first candle. Then she hesitated, glancing through the open window at the road just outside.

"Let's close the windows and shutters first," she said quietly. "So nobody can overhear us singing in Hebrew. It's better if nobody here knows for sure that we're Jewish."

She blew out the match, and she and Gustave and Papa closed the shutters in the kitchen and living room and latched the windows. The rooms were suddenly dark and somber again.

They gathered around the table, and Maman again lifted the shawl over her head, lit the candles, and closed her eyes. In her clear, high voice, she sang the Hebrew blessing over the candles. She sang more quietly than she usually did, and Gustave heard a slight quaver. Papa stood beside Maman, solid and calm. His voice was warm and rich when he and Gustave joined in to chant the Sabbath prayers. Gustave watched their faces in the glow of the candlelight, singing the blessing over the wine, singing the blessing over the bread.

"Shabbat shalom," said Papa and Maman and Gustave to each other when they had finished. "A Sabbath of peace."

But even though it was Shabbat, and despite what Papa had said earlier, Maman had two small worry lines between her eyes. A Sabbath of peace, thought Gustave, remembering Maman's earlier words about Saint-Georges. A peaceful place. But would Saint-Georges really turn out to be a safe place, a place of peace? Looking at the shutters hiding them from the street, and remembering the snarling dog and the blank face of the boy with the pale eyes, Gustave didn't feel sure of that. Not sure at all.

6

Saint-Georges, April 1940

Gustave had been in Saint-Georges for three long weeks. Late one Tuesday afternoon in April, with his rucksack on his back, he pulled himself up into his fort in the loft of the garage and threw down the three long, sturdy sticks he was holding. Madame Foncine wouldn't let Gustave explore the attic, but she hadn't said anything about staying out of the garage—not that Gustave had asked her, exactly. He knew better than to do that, after what she had said about boys messing around in her attic. So Gustave slipped in and out of the garage when she wasn't watching. The old building had once been a barn, and it had a hayloft at one end that made a perfect fort.

Gustave looked around in satisfaction. He had spread a khaki blanket over the splintery floor and arranged three bales of hay in a triangle for seats. If Jean-Paul and Marcel came to join Gustave in Saint-Georges, the fort would be all ready for the three of them. There were two lookout windows facing in different directions.

"Perfect for spying on the enemy," Gustave said to himself. "If the Boches ever dare come here."

He took out his pocketknife and began sharpening the first of the three long sticks that he had found in the yard behind the house. When he had made three spears, one for each boy, he arranged the weapons against the wall. In his rucksack were the Y-shaped stick he had found last week and an old pair of underwear. Yesterday he had torn them so badly when they caught on a twig while he was climbing one of the hazelnut trees that Maman had said they couldn't be mended. Now he carefully cut the elastic off with his pocketknife and attached it to the Y-shaped stick, making a perfect slingshot. He shoved it into his back pocket.

"Just in case," he muttered.

In Gustave's opinion, the fort was the best thing about Saint-Georges. Otherwise, it was lonely. Luckily, he had never run into the pale-eyed boy again, but he also hadn't found anyone else to hang around with. He wasn't going to school. Papa said that it didn't make much sense to go, since the school year was nearly over, and they might not be in Saint-Georges very long. Once, at the post office, Gustave had spotted the little boy who had peered out at him from the gate that first day, and another time, Gustave had seen a group of girls about his age in the village. One girl had looked at him curiously, but it was hard just to go up and start talking to girls you didn't know. Maman was away from home a lot now, working at a typing job she had found almost right away. She pedaled off in the mornings on an old bicycle she had bought from Madame Foncine.

Without his store, Papa didn't have much to do in Saint-Georges either. He listened to the radio a lot, and sometimes he and Gustave worked together, fixing things in the new house. Sometimes he walked to nearby villages and sat in cafés for hours, talking with other men about the war. The house was often empty. Gustave would never admit it to Jean-Paul, and especially not to Marcel, but these days, he usually carried Monkey around in his pocket, just to have a little company.

Gustave climbed down from the loft and wandered into the kitchen. Maman was home from work early, and she had a box of photographs open on the table. She was sorting them into piles while dinner simmered on the stove.

"Look, Gustave," Maman said, smiling. "Here's a picture of you when you were a baby. Do you remember this little tricycle you used to ride? And look—here is one of you and Marcel, eating your first ice cream cones ever!"

Gustave looked over her shoulder and laughed. In the ice cream picture, Marcel was standing and Gustave was in a stroller. Both of them were grinning, their faces and shirts covered in chocolate.

"Do you have a newer one of me and Marcel and Jean-Paul?" Gustave asked. "One I can put in the picture frame that's in my room?"

"Oh, I'm sure there's one in there somewhere," Maman said, getting up from her seat to check on the pot on the stove. "Go ahead and look. Just be sure to hold the photos by their edges so that you don't get fingerprints on them."

Gustave went up to get the frame and came back down, rubbing the dull metal on his shirt to make it shiny. He sat at the table and shuffled through the photographs. He found one of Maman and Aunt Geraldine as teenagers, smiling astride their bicycles, and one of Papa with a much younger Gustave on his shoulders. There was Papa as a boy, standing waist-deep with his friends in a lake in Switzerland, snow-capped mountains soaring behind them.

"Oh, look—perfect!" Gustave cried. Maman leaned over his shoulder to see a photo of Gustave, Marcel, and Jean-Paul on their winter camping trip in the mountains two years ago. Gustave and Jean-Paul were bundled up, but Marcel had stripped off his hat, jacket, and shirt for the photograph and was standing bare-chested in the snow, flexing his arm muscles to show how tough he was. The three of them were standing close together, laughing.

The photograph fit perfectly into the frame. Holding it against his chest, Gustave walked upstairs. He put it down slowly on the night table. Maybe he would see his friends again soon. The way things were going with the war, it sounded as if they would need to come to Saint-Georges after all.

Gustave glanced over his shoulder at the map on his wall, then quickly looked away. There was an awful lot of red on it now. A week ago, the Nazis had launched a surprise attack on Denmark and Norway, so now Denmark was red too. Denmark's army was so small that it hadn't even tried to fight back. Now Norway was fighting the Germans.

When the news of Norway's entry into the war had come, Maman had gone straight to the post office to telephone her sister. Aunt Geraldine had said that she would think again about coming to live in the countryside. She had also promised to talk to Madame Landau, Marcel's mother, since the Landaus didn't have a telephone.

"We could easily find a cheap place for Geraldine to rent here," Maman said to Papa. "And I told her to tell the Landaus that they can stay with us if they can't afford a place of their own. Surely, now that they see what is happening, they will come soon."

"Since Aunt Geraldine hates outhouses, you should just tell her that some of the houses here have bathrooms," Gustave suggested. "That way she won't have any reason not to come."

Maman laughed. "I'm not sure that any of them really do have bathrooms. But it's a good idea. I'll tell her next time I call."

But whatever Maman had said to Aunt Geraldine, days passed and still Jean-Paul's family and the Landaus did not come. And every night on the news broadcast, the radio announcer talked about the war. "Aided by the British navy, Norway fights valiantly!" the broadcaster announced, as Gustave and his parents listened to the radio that evening after dinner. "King Haakon rejects Nazi demands!"

The radio announcer always sounded so certain that the Nazis would soon be beaten, Gustave thought as he put on his pajamas. But when was it going to happen? The Nazis

50

had taken over so many other countries. What was happening now to all the people in the occupied countries, to ordinary, nice people like his family who just wanted to live their lives?

Another thought came into Gustave's mind, so quietly that it was like a whisper, insistent and taunting, making his temples throb. If the Nazis hated Jews so much, what was happening to the Jews in those countries that they had taken over? Were those prison camps for Jews and other people the Nazis didn't like just in Poland, or in all the defeated countries? And when would they let the people in them out?

Downstairs, Maman was listening to a symphony on the radio as she cleaned up the kitchen. The music, drifting up from below, suddenly sounded unbearably sad. Gustave closed his door, but he could still hear the muffled notes. He threw himself down on the bed, squeezing a pillow against each side of his head to block out the sound.

"Shut up, shut up, shut up!" he muttered into the mattress, not sure whether he was talking to the whispers in his head or to the radio. He lay there in the dark, his head buried in the pillows, trying to sleep, but he could still hear the melancholy strains of the music. It was a long time before Maman switched the radio off.

7

One warm morning in May, Madame Foncine shuffled by the wide-open shutters while Gustave and his parents were eating breakfast, and a moment later she banged loudly on the front door.

"Now, finally, we are going to start fighting back against the Boches," she announced, her broad face flushed with excitement. "Our war has begun. The Germans have invaded Holland, Belgium, and Luxembourg."

Gustave's mouth felt dry. Luxembourg and Belgium were between France and Germany. That meant that now the Nazis were heading right toward France.

Gustave's family was quiet as Madame Foncine walked away. Then Maman leaned against Papa and sighed.

"Oh, why won't Geraldine see that she should leave Paris?" she moaned into Papa's chest.

"Well, at least the waiting is over," Papa said, stroking her hair. "Now the French army can start pushing the Germans back."

But that wasn't what happened. On Monday evening, Papa turned on the radio after dinner. It crackled, making Gustave jump. A somber voice spoke into the room.

"German tanks have crossed the Meuse River from Belgium and penetrated France," boomed the announcer. "There is fierce fighting in the French region of Sedan."

Gustave felt hollowed out inside. The Nazis were in France. Was it possible? For a moment, he could hardly breathe. The room swirled around him, and a roaring sound filled his ears. When his head quieted, Maman and Papa were talking.

"*When* will we hear about those visas?" Maman cried, hugging herself with both arms and rocking back and forth on the sofa.

Papa paced, limping up and down the room. "Maybe we should leave for Switzerland instead of waiting to hear about emigrating to America," he said.

"But Geraldine and her family will never be able to cross the Swiss border to meet us there," Maman wailed. "And what if Germany decides to invade Switzerland? What should we do? Oh, what should we do?"

"Be calm, Lili *chérie,* be calm," Papa said. "The Germans are only slightly over our border. General Weygand has established a second front. The second front is holding."

But day after day, the names of the countries collapsing in front of the German army came on the news bulletins, solemn and funereal, like a church bell tolling. "Luxembourg offers no resistance." "Holland surrenders." When would the Nazis stop? Gustave wondered as he painted in the fallen countries on his map.

He was washing paint over Luxembourg when his hand jerked, and a smear of red slid onto the blue of France. Gustave wiped at it furiously with his handkerchief until it was clean, then clenched the brush tightly so that he wouldn't slip and get any more red where it didn't belong. After all, the Nazis hadn't taken over the whole world.

France was still free.

Days passed, and the fields turned a darker shade of green. Flowers budded and opened, and, even at night, the air was soft and warm, like the fuzzy skin of a peach. One night after the news broadcast, Gustave could smell spring in the air as he walked upstairs with heavy feet. But the weather felt all wrong. How could spring come the same way it always did? Under his open bedroom window, the garden was full of flowers, and birds were singing as the sun set. But Gustave felt separated from the warm night, as if it were all happening on the other side of a wall of glass. He flipped open the metal water-color box and looked down at his paints. He had plenty of all the other colors, but in the center of the well of red paint, he could see the metal at the bottom. And again, tonight, red was the color he needed. Belgium had surrendered to the Nazis.

Gustave swirled the wet brush around in the paint and slowly washed red over Belgium. When he was finished, he studied the map in bewilderment. Red was spreading like blood all over Europe, even along much of the French border.

And, still, the strange spring kept on coming. One hot June morning, Gustave woke up late, tangled in sticky sheets. Voices were coming from outside. He stumbled downstairs, but neither of his parents was in the house, and the front door stood open.

"Papa?" he called out. "Maman?"

Still half-asleep, he walked out into the yard. The paving stones under his bare feet were already warm, almost hot, from the sunshine. Out in the road, five or six adults he didn't know and a few small children stood huddled in a tight group. A woman ran down the street toward them, her hair disheveled, her dress flapping around her legs, screaming. Gustave watched her lips moving. He heard the sounds, but at first the words didn't make sense. "They're coming! The Germans! They're coming! The Germans!"

The woman's husband pulled her toward him, and a small child let out a high, piercing cry.

A rush of energy swept over Gustave, leaving him sweaty, then cold an instant later. He heard a noise behind him and turned. Papa had taken the truck out. The back, still filled with stock from the Paris store, was open. Papa ran, limping unevenly, out of the garage, toward the truck, a spare can of gasoline sloshing in each hand. Light glinted off the truck and the cans of gasoline. Gustave darted toward Papa. "Are the Germans really coming?" he cried.

"Yes!" Papa shouted. "The Nazis have bombed Paris. The second front has collapsed. Help Maman grab some clothes and food. We have to get out of here. *Now*."

8

The Exodus, June 1940

Gustave leaned forward in the front seat of the truck, pulling his damp shirt away from his back, bewildered by what he saw through the windshield of the truck. Papa had driven at breakneck speed through the roads leading out of the village. But now that they were on the highway, the space ahead of them was so jammed with vehicles and people, all heading in the same direction, that the truck was barely moving. Heat shimmered in the air. Cars and trucks overloaded with passengers clogged the road, honking. People shouted and horses whinnied, pulling heavy farm wagons piled high with mattresses and furniture. Men and women on bicycles wove in and out. Others walked, pushing wheelbarrows and baby carriages, some with babies and children in them, clinging to the sides, their eyes wide.

One man had fixed a strap across his own chest as if he

were a donkey. Leaning forward, with sweat running down his face, step by step, he pulled a cart in which a frail, elderly woman sat, clutching a baby on her lap. People trudged along the side of the road on foot, their heads down, lugging bags and suitcases. A young woman sat on her suitcase by the side of the road, her eyes dull. Two small children with runny noses clung to her, wailing. The air was thick with dust stirred up by tires, by the feet of people, and by the hooves of horses. Exhaust fumes hung in the heavy air.

Where Gustave's shorts ended, the rough seat of the delivery truck made his bare legs itch. They were driving so slowly that almost no breeze came in through the wide-open windows.

"Where are we going?" Gustave asked suddenly. "Are we going to Switzerland?"

"No. The Germans might cut us off before we got there," said Papa, staring ahead at the clogged road. "We're heading south, away from the Germans. We're going to try to make it into Spain."

"If they haven't closed the border," said Maman, who was squeezed in the middle. Her voice sounded thin, breakable. "At some point the Spaniards will say enough is enough, if mobs of people like this keep trying to get in."

Gustave looked around the slow-moving crowd. "Are all of these people Jewish?" he asked. He hadn't known that there were so many Jews in all of France put together.

Papa stopped trying to pass a huge, slow-moving hay wagon with eleven people, mostly children, seated against its railings, and sighed, craning his neck out the window and trying to see around the wagon.

"What did you say, Gustave?" he asked when he pulled his head back in. "Are they all Jewish? No. Maybe some of them. But anyone with any sense wants to get away from the Germans," he added bitterly. "Everyone has heard what the Boches have done in other countries. Shootings, burning down villages—"

"Berthold!" Maman put her hand on Papa's arm to stop him. But Gustave had heard enough. His pulse throbbed painfully in his throat. The Germans were marching through France, heading toward Paris. He couldn't imagine it. What was happening to Marcel and Jean-Paul and their families? Had their apartment building been bombed? Were German tanks rolling through the streets? It seemed so unreal to think of soldiers with guns in front of the movie theaters and the shops full of bright flowers. Were soldiers ducking down to shoot from behind café tables and the bookstalls along the Seine? Gustave reached into his pocket and clutched Monkey. If only it were still last year instead of this one, and he and Marcel and Jean-Paul were safely together in the park in Paris, the light slanting down through the trees, as they stood together on the stone wall, about to jump, pretending they were spies parachuting out of an airplane.

"Papa," Gustave asked, his voice wobbly, "where do you think Marcel and Jean-Paul . . . ?"

Papa glanced at Maman. She was staring fixedly out the window, her face white. "Enough questions, Gustave," he said. "We'll talk about that later."

Gustave turned and put his arm on the open window of the truck. He rested his head on it, and in a daze, he watched the mass of people outside. What was Jean-Paul doing? Was Aunt Geraldine rushing desperately through the streets in her high heels, perfume, and an elegant dress, pushing Giselle in her baby carriage, with Jean-Paul running beside her, the gas masks swinging from his shoulder? What about Marcel and his mother? Were they running away, or crouching in their apartment, peering out the window? The images in his head came so fast that Gustave felt as if he were spinning around until the world became a sickening blur.

At lunchtime, Papa stopped to get the food out of the back. Gustave and Maman got out to stretch for a moment. Gustave stood up unsteadily. The sun beat down, hot on his head, and between the sounds of motors, he heard insects buzzing over the fields. He and Papa and Maman ate bread and cheese as the truck moved slowly back into the stream of traffic. Gustave tilted his head back and drank the last, warm swallow of water in the canteen Maman handed him.

"That is the end of our food, Berthold," Maman said, her voice tight.

"Don't worry," answered Papa. "We'll stop in the next town and buy some."

It was late afternoon when they rolled slowly into a town. For hours, Gustave's mouth had felt dry and sticky, and by now, his stomach ached with hunger. Maman banged on the door of two bakeries and tried a shop that sold cheese, one that sold meat and sausages, and one that sold vegetables. But the bakeries were closed, and the other shopkeepers had empty shelves.

"Nothing?" Maman asked the woman who kept the vegetable shop, her voice trembling. Her face was drawn and exhausted. "Not a single potato? Not even an onion? Not a single bouillon cube to make soup? You have nothing at all to sell?"

"Not since about noon today," said the shopkeeper. "People have been coming through here like locusts."

"Would you give us some water?" asked Maman, showing her the empty canteen.

The shopkeeper had a round, grandmotherly face. She nodded and went to her house behind the store. She came back with a jug of water and a tall, creamy glass of milk.

"For the young one," she said. She wouldn't take the money Maman offered. Gustave squirmed when the shopkeeper handed him the glass. He wasn't so young. He was a Boy Scout, and he was supposed to help others. He gulped down one-third of the milk. It was hard to stop, but one-third was his fair share. He held out the glass to Maman. She shook her head.

"Please?" he said. "Papa?"

Neither of them would take the glass. Looking at their faces, Gustave could see that they weren't going to change their minds. He gulped down the rest while Papa and Maman watched. Even with the milk in his stomach, he still felt painfully hungry.

As the sky over the fields grew darker, Papa started looking for somewhere where they could spend the night.

"Shouldn't we keep on as long as we can?" asked Maman, twisting her hands in her lap.

"Oh, you think so?" Papa snapped.

Gustave looked at him, startled. Papa never got angry like that.

"How would we look from above, with our headlights on?"

"Oh. Yes." Maman turned her head, staring back out the window.

Papa stopped the truck beside a field where many other travelers had set up camp. Some people were already sleeping on the grass or under wagons. One large family nearby was cooking soup over a camp stove. The scent of chicken, carrots, and potatoes drifted in the air. The smells made Gustave's stomach twist painfully again. If Maman had been able to buy an onion, he could have made a campfire, and she could have prepared onion soup. Gustave wanted onion soup so badly that he could almost taste it. The glass of milk he had drunk seemed very far away. His head ached, and he rubbed his fingers over his eyebrows and into his temples, trying to press away the pain. His arms and legs felt strangely weightless, as if he might float away into the rapidly cooling air.

"I'll go knock at some doors and see if any of the farmers around here will sell us some food," Papa said. He walked away with the up-and-down, limping walk that Gustave would know anywhere, toward the dark shape of a farmhouse, getting smaller and smaller, silhouetted against the deep blue of the sky. When he was out of sight, Gustave shivered. The air felt thinner with Papa gone.

"Let's set up camp," said Maman. She was trying to be cheerful, but Gustave knew she hated camping.

Gustave pulled out the blankets and pillows Maman

had thrown into the truck that morning and arranged them on the grass. Maman sat down on the red plaid blanket, pulling her sweater around her shoulders and gazing in the direction Papa had gone. All at once, Gustave was exhausted. He lay down on the green blanket with his jacket over him. The ground was cold and lumpy through the thin wool.

Overhead, in the peaceful night sky, the stars were coming out. Somewhere else in the field, a baby was crying. Gustave let his eyes close and his mind drift. It was almost like going camping with the Boy Scouts, he thought sleepily. Almost. If Jean-Paul and Marcel were lying next to him in sleeping bags. If only they really were. He imagined the three families camping together, the parents sitting by a campfire, Aunt Geraldine holding the baby, while he and his friends whispered in the shadows. It would be fun, doing that together. If they had enough food. And if they weren't running away.

9

When Gustave opened his eyes, he blinked, confused for a moment, at the dark shapes around him and at the sky, growing lighter behind the silhouettes of the trees. He sat up, rubbing his shoulder where it was sore from pressing into the hard ground. A mosquito bite throbbed on his ankle, and then other places started itching, on his forehead, his neck, and his arm. He scratched, and the mosquito bites felt better, then burned again, itchy and hot. Maman was already sitting up on the blanket, smoothing her hair. Papa groaned and rolled over in his sleep, then sat up, awake in an instant. He stood and stretched, walked over to the truck, unlocked the front door, and pulled out a loaf of bread and some cheese he had bought from a farmer the night before.

"We waited to eat with you this morning, Gustave," Maman said. "You were asleep when Papa got back."

They all tore off a piece of bread, and Maman handed each of them a sliver of cheese. "We need to save some for later," she said. "We may not be able to buy any more today."

"Enjoy this food," Papa said wryly. "It ought to be good. It's the most expensive loaf of bread I've ever bought. That farmer charged me three times the usual price."

Nearby, four children sat on a bed of hay in a farm wagon, sharing a long sausage. Gustave watched them while he chewed on his bread. The oldest child, a girl about Gustave's age, ate her piece of sausage quickly and tended to a pony that was tethered nearby. First she brought him hay and water; then she brushed him. The pony was beautiful, chestnut-colored and sturdy, with a pale mane and deep brown eyes. When Gustave finished his hunk of bread and the small morsel of cheese, he got up and walked a few steps closer to watch.

The girl looked up from grooming the pony and smiled. "His name is Jacques," she said. "He's mine. Do you want to pet him?"

Gustave reached out and stroked the pony's coarse mane, touching lightly at first, then wriggling his fingers in deep. The pony turned his head and nuzzled Gustave's shoulder, tickling him with his warm, moist breath. "He's hoping you have food for him," said the girl.

"No. I wish I did," said Gustave. "I'd eat it!"

The girl laughed. "Even if it was hay?"

Gustave grinned back. "Maybe. I'm almost hungry enough."

"Gustave," called his mother. "We're leaving! Now!"

"I have to go," Gustave said. "Maybe I'll see you and Jacques later on the road." The girl nodded and went back to brushing the pony.

The highway was as crowded with people and cars and trucks and farm wagons as it had been the day before.

"Are we almost there?" Gustave asked.

Papa laughed shortly. "We only went about forty kilometers yesterday," he said. "It's going to take us many days at this rate."

"Many days?" Gustave groaned. He was already fidgety from sitting still so long, and he was hungry again too. His stomach felt like an impatient animal, ravenous so soon after eating. How could they possibly go on like this for many days, especially if they couldn't buy any more food? The air was stifling in the cab of the truck, heavy with exhaust fumes from the slow-moving traffic. Gustave's throat was very dry. "Can I have some water?" he asked.

"Just a few sips," said Maman, handing him the canteen Papa had refilled at the farm. "We need to save the rest for later."

Gustave sighed. If he could fill his stomach with water, maybe it wouldn't gnaw at him so much, but they didn't even have enough water. It was obvious that it was going to be another long day. Gustave rubbed his mosquito bites.

"Don't scratch," said Papa absently. "It makes it worse."

How was he supposed to do *that*? The bite on Gustave's arm was getting red and swollen. He pressed his fingernail down over it hard one way and then the other, making an X to cross out the pain. There, that wasn't scratching, and it made the itchiness go away, at least temporarily. A loud honking was coming closer. Gustave looked up from his itchy arm and noticed that a few of the vehicles and people were shifting over to the side of the road, although most of them stayed where they were. A French soldier strode through the slow-moving crowd, heading in the opposite direction.

"Clear the way," he shouted impatiently. "Army vehicles coming through."

"Finally, we see some of our own soldiers," Papa said, pulling over, "and people won't get out of their way. Idiots." Papa's unshaven face looked tired and grim.

Eventually, the crowd gave way a bit, and several trucks full of French soldiers drove through slowly, honking. In one truck, three of the soldiers had binoculars pressed against their eyes and were scanning the sky. One of the soldiers saw Gustave watching and saluted him, smiling.

Gustave put his hands up to his eyes, wondering what it was like to look through army binoculars. As the trucks full of soldiers passed, Papa maneuvered his way back into the flow of traffic. Gustave scanned the crowd, looking through his imaginary hand binoculars. Did putting your hands to your eyes like that make things look closer? It almost seemed as if it did, especially when he closed his fingers in the middle, making two circles. Gustave looked through his hands at the tops of the trees on the side of the road, at clouds in the sky, at the hat of a man walking by the side of the road.

From time to time, Gustave spotted the girl with the pony. When she saw him, she waved, and he waved back.

Jacques, wearing blinders, was tethered next to another pony, helping to pull a wagon loaded down with four children, a grandfather clock, and a heavy wooden bed frame. Gustave felt weary just watching the small ponies straining to pull the weight. It looked like really hard, hot work, even though the grown-ups of the family were walking beside the cart and the oldest girl often got out and walked next to Jacques with her hand on his neck.

Once, when they came into view on the road, she called to Gustave, who was now hanging out the window, "Come on out and walk with us!"

Gustave could see that there was a breeze outside. "Can I get out and walk for a while?" he asked. "We aren't going any faster than that, anyway."

"No!" said Maman sharply. "We don't want to lose you."

"I'm not going to get lost," Gustave protested. "I'm *eleven.*"

Maman didn't answer, and Gustave slammed himself back against the seat. How could anyone get lost? Everyone except for the soldiers was heading in the same direction, down the same endless road. The worst thing about the day wasn't being hungry or hot or thirsty. It was having nothing to do. If only Jean-Paul or Marcel were there for him to poke or talk to or play rock-paper-scissors with. Gustave felt a heavy weight on his chest. He didn't want to think about where Jean-Paul and Marcel might be right now. Instead, he tried playing rock-paper-scissors with himself, one hand against the other, but it didn't work very well. Somehow, he always let the left hand win.

Gustave gave up and looked at the green fields stretching

out on either side of the road, and then up into the sky. A buzzard hung in the hot air above the endless column of people on the road, circling, its wings in a V. Gustave put his hands up into the binocular shape again to watch the buzzard wheeling through the sky. Suddenly, a dark object appeared on the horizon behind the buzzard, then another, and another. Gustave moved his hand binoculars over to look at them more closely. Planes. Painted with dark crosses and swastikas. For a moment, Gustave's mouth wouldn't work. Then he shouted, "Planes! Nazi planes!"

"Pull over!" Maman screamed. The planes roared down through the sky, straight toward the column of people on the road, as if they were going to land on top of them. It sounded as if the sky were tearing in two. Through the roar came the wails of babies and the high, shrieking whinny of horses. People ran in every direction.

Gustave pushed the door open while the truck was still moving.

"Run!" Papa shouted. Gustave stumbled across the rutted field, his breath tearing through his lungs, making for a line of trees. Maman was to the side of him, but Papa, limping on his bad leg, was falling behind. Gustave turned around and reached out a hand to help him, but Papa waved him away, screaming, "Run!"

The machine guns began just as Gustave reached the trees. Glancing up, he saw a plane no higher than the tree-tops, its machine gun pointing down. Bullets exploded. Hands shoved Gustave to the ground as Papa threw himself over him, heavy and solid, shielding Gustave from the cruel sky. Gustave's heart was hammering, and his breath came in gasps. His lip bled where his teeth had cut it, and his blood tasted like metal. His cheek pressed against a bumpy tree root. His nose was full of the smell of the damp earth and the familiar scent of his father's shirt.

After a long while, the noise of the shooting stopped. Gustave could feel Papa's heart pounding against his back. He heard the thrumming rising from the earth and the insects humming over the field. But he didn't want Papa to get up. He wanted to stay there forever, wedged safely between the warmth of Papa's body and the cool, damp ground.

When Papa finally did push himself to his hands and knees, Gustave lifted his head and saw that Maman was next to them, holding Papa's arm.

The heel had broken off one of Maman's shoes, and her left stocking was torn. Her breathing was ragged and hoarse. "Oh, Gustave!" she gasped, reaching for him. "Oh, Berthold!"

With Maman limping on the broken shoe, they made their way back across the rutted field. It was the same brilliantly sunny day it had been an hour ago, but it was as if the familiar world had been turned upside down and shaken into a new pattern, like bits of colored glass in a kaleidoscope. People were scattered around, some still screaming, others weeping. Some crawled out of the ditches beside the road and from under trucks and cars. Windshields had shattered. The road sparkled with broken glass. An elegant elderly woman sat in a ditch, her face dirty and her hat awry, looking stunned. A small boy, all by himself and too young to talk, stood crying forlornly. Maman paused and snapped the heel off her other shoe so that she could balance. She knelt down beside the little boy, wiping his nose with her handkerchief.

"Shhh," she told him, taking his hand. "We'll find your mother."

"Maybe she's over there," said Gustave shakily, pointing toward a stone structure on the other side of the road where some people had run for shelter. Together, his family and the little boy made their way toward it. The ground was covered with dropped objects: a broken-handled suitcase, a sweater, a doll, one leg doubled under its body, gazing up at the sky with green glass eyes.

When they had almost reached the shed, a bedraggled young woman hurried toward them, weeping wildly, carrying a baby and clutching a little girl by the hand. The boy cried out and rushed toward her.

"He pulled and ran off," the mother said over and over again to Maman, embracing her. "I couldn't hold on to him." The mother wept, but the boy, holding her skirt with one hand and sucking his thumb on the other, had stopped crying and was looking around, his eyes enormous. Gustave followed the boy's gaze and looked out over the field. In the distance, under the bright glare of the sky, some people were still lying on the grass, unmoving.

"Don't look, Gustave," said Papa sharply. "Let's get going." He stepped between Gustave and the field, blocking his view, and, with his arm around Gustave's shoulder, turned him in the direction of the road.

Gustave saw the delivery truck. It was like suddenly seeing home. "There it is!" he cried, running forward.

"Be careful of the broken glass!" Maman called.

No bullets had gone through the windshield of the truck. But there was something large and dark lying beside it in the road.

"Wait!" Gustave's mother caught him from behind, but he shrugged her off and darted forward. It was Jacques, the pony. He had been shot. His beautiful brown head was thrown back, and a pool of dark blood spread out around him. His pale mane was stained where it lay in the blood. The girl Gustave had talked to that morning sat on the ground beside Jacques, her arms around him, crying, her hair falling over her face. Gustave's stomach clenched. He took a few steps toward the bushes on the side of the road and threw up.

"Barbarians," Papa muttered when they were back in the truck. "Barbarians."

The road was jammed again with exhausted, desperate people. Gustave curled up on the seat and put his head down on his knees. He couldn't stop seeing the dead pony. His chest started to shudder, gasping for breath, and his eyes leaked tears. After a while, he felt Maman's hand on his back. He could hear her crying too.

"We're going to be all right, Gustave," said Papa hoarsely. "We will keep our family safe." But how could Papa be sure of that? And what about Marcel and Jean-Paul and their families? After a long time, Gustave's tears stopped. His eyes were swollen and hot, his mind empty. They drove on, slowly, for hours and hours. Around night-fall, the road was in complete confusion. Traffic stopped entirely.

Gustave's father got out of the truck to see what was happening.

"A bomb exploded up ahead," said a man on foot, his shoulders sagging under a heavy rucksack. His face was lined, and his eyes were sunken. "It destroyed the bridge and killed quite a few people. No one can get past."

Papa's face was grim. With difficulty, he turned the truck around. The stream of people began slowly walking the other way, heading back in the direction from which they had come.

"What do you think?" Papa said to Maman. "We could take another route, but in this mess, we won't get to Spain for days. It's obvious that the Germans are deliberately trying to kill civilians on the highways. It seems more dangerous on the road than anywhere else. And we may well be turned back at the Spanish border even if we get there."

Maman nodded slowly. "And we have so little food, and we may not be able to find more. Or more gasoline. If we go on, we might end up stranded somewhere. Let's go back to Saint-Georges," she said quietly.

Gustave sat up. He hadn't said anything for a long time, and his throat was dry. "But won't the Germans be in Saint-Georges?" he whispered hoarsely.

"I'm hoping that they won't bother going into such a tiny village," said Papa. His voice was weary. "But they may be."

10

Saint-Georges, June 1940

It took almost three more days to get home. On the way
back, they passed a town that had been bombed. The
black skeletons of buildings reached up into the quiet sky.
They drove by abandoned automobiles with flat tires and
others that must have run out of gasoline. Flies buzzed over
another dead horse at the side of the road, next to a wagon
with a broken wheel. Gustave also saw bags and suitcases,
a cooking pot, a clock, and a teddy bear, all things that people must have dropped when they got too heavy to carry.

When Papa drove the truck back into Saint-Georges, it
was late in the afternoon. The old stone house stood as it
had for a hundred years, quiet and solid, behind its low wall.
Gustave took the box his father handed him and trudged
toward the door. Some men walked over to help Papa

unload and to ask what they had seen. Gustave was too tired to talk to anyone.

The first few days back, he slept a lot of the time. Maman returned to her job. Two other families from the village, as well as several young men who feared being recruited into the German army, had left the same day that their family had, she reported when she came home. But they had all returned already, discouraged by the impossible traffic. No one had seen any Germans in the area yet, she said.

But there was other news that Gustave and his family had missed while they were on the road. After a month of hard fighting, Norway had surrendered to the Nazis. Gustave overheard Monsieur Grégoire, the elderly man who lived across the road, telling Papa about it as they both stood, grim-faced, in the street one morning. That night, Gustave slowly painted Norway red on his map. His thoughts were fuzzy, and it took a long time for him to do anything, as if his brain weren't connected quite right to his body. He stared at the open watercolor box.

The red paint was nearly gone, and the block of blue paint was almost untouched. Nazi tanks were on French soil, and their planes were in the sky over France. And he and Maman and Papa couldn't get out. They were caught like rabbits waiting, trembling, in a trap.

The next morning, Gustave was tying a long rope to one of the rafters by the open window of his fort to make an emergency exit, when he saw something unfamiliar glinting on the road in the distance. A faint rhythmical pounding was getting louder and louder.

He hurried down the ladder and ran to the gate to see what was going on. A woman emerged from the house across the street, wiping her hands on her apron. Other people opened the doors of their houses and stood watching over the walls and along the sides of the road. The pounding came closer, and then Gustave heard hooves. A man riding a glossy black horse appeared at the bottom of the hill. Gustave stared, but what he saw didn't change. The man had a rifle slung over his shoulder, and he was wearing a German uniform.

The horse tossed its head and started up the hill. More soldiers straddling muscular horses followed. The hooves clopped up the road, right in front of Gustave's house. Behind the men on horseback came marching German soldiers, wave after wave of them, as if they would keep on coming forever. Gustave watched the shiny black boots. Eighty-two, eighty-four, eighty-six, eighty-eight, he counted feverishly. If he could only count fast enough, he thought dazedly, he would know how many there were. Ninety, ninety-two, ninety-four, ninety-six. But the boots, rising up and smashing down, swam in front of him, and he lost count. He dragged his eyes away and looked up. Greenish gray uniforms, steel helmets, rifles. Faces like stone. The soldiers looked straight ahead as they marched south, turned the corner, and disappeared out of sight. They seemed to know exactly where they were going. They moved like machines, not men.

Some of the watching French men and women wept silently, tears running down their faces. Gustave could hear his heart pounding, more loudly than the thunderous marching boots. He felt frozen to the ground, unable to move or even to turn his eyes away from the soldiers. German soldiers were marching through the streets of France, his country, his native land. Marching right through this tiny country village, this little, out-of-the-way place, where his family had come to be safe. It was like a nightmare. It couldn't be real. But it was.

A few houses away, on the other side of the road, two huge, wolflike dogs leapt at the gate from inside, snarling and growling. Their owner, Monsieur Grégoire, leaned on the wall across the road, his face twisted with grief. Let them out, Gustave thought despairingly. Let out the *chiens méchants*!

But of course Monsieur Grégoire wouldn't do that. Even if those dogs, with their fierce teeth, managed to hurt a few soldiers, the other Germans would just take their rifles down off their shoulders and shoot them. They would probably shoot Monsieur Grégoire too. The waves of Germans marched up the road, as the French people stood watching, and, over and over again, the dogs hurled themselves uselessly against the gate.

When the first tank rumbled up the road, Gustave couldn't watch anymore. There were too many soldiers. Too many tanks. He ran away from the road and, on his hands and knees, pushed his way under the low branches, into the bushes behind the garage. He sat there, curled up in the tight space, for a long time, trying to stop shaking. When he crawled out, all the tanks seemed to have rumbled by, but he could hear more feet marching.

He scrambled up the ladder to the loft and looked

around. The three spears still leaned against the wall, at the ready. He flushed. They didn't look like spears anymore, just like stupid sharpened sticks. Dumb toys. And he was all by himself. Marcel and Jean-Paul weren't there. Maybe they never would be. What did he think he needed three sharpened sticks for? He seized the spears angrily and cracked them over his knee, one after the other, until all that was left of them was a mess of splintered wood.

The sound of the marching German boots gradually faded away into the distance, going deeper and deeper into France.

11

"A large part of our territory will be occupied on a temporary basis," said an unfamiliar voice on the radio. It was Maréchal Pétain, who had just been appointed the new leader of France.

"Armistice!" Papa shouted back at the radio when the speech was over. "That's what you call an armistice! Appalling."

"What does it mean?" Gustave jumped to his feet and grabbed Papa's arm. "What's happening?"

"It is a national disgrace!" Papa stormed. "This Maréchal Pétain has surrendered to the Germans, and he's just sitting back and taking orders from them!"

"It means that France has stopped fighting the war," Maman explained. "So the Germans won't be shooting at

French people from airplanes anymore or dropping bombs."

"Sure!" Papa snorted. "But Pétain is going to let the Nazis occupy a large part of France. And who knows what they'll do. Especially to the Jews."

"But what *part* is going to be occupied?" cried Gustave.

"Let's go," said Maman. She and Papa were already at the front door. "We're going to get a newspaper and find out."

The papers were all sold out in Saint-Georges, so they hurried the few kilometers to the nearby village of Francueil. Papa bought a newspaper and an ice-cold lemonade, and the three of them sat at a rickety black metal table in the tiny café to share the lemonade and study the map in the paper. At one of the other two tables, an elderly couple pored over another paper, ignoring their breakfast. A pigeon waddled close to their table, pecked up a large crumb, then fluttered away.

"Look," Papa said after hastily examining the blurry map in the paper and tracing a line with his finger. "Saint-Georges is just south of the demarcation line between the occupied zone and the unoccupied zone. Ah!" he breathed, slapping both hands on the table and looking at Maman. "What incredible luck! We're in the unoccupied zone!"

Maman pulled the map toward her. "Incredible!" she murmured. "What if the house we had rented had been just on the other side of the river?"

"So there won't be any Germans here?" Gustave leaned over Maman's shoulder.

"No. It says that they have all withdrawn to the northern part of the country," Papa answered. "The new French Vichy government, headed by Maréchal Pétain, is in charge here, in the unoccupied zone."

"Oh!" Maman pushed the paper away and put her head down in her hands. "But Paris will be occupied."

"Of course they want Paris," Papa exploded, looking at her incredulously. "What did you think?"

"I thought they might just want to take back Alsace and Lorraine," said Maman, gesturing toward the regions of France closest to Germany, her voice tremulous. "The Boches always thought Alsace and Lorraine should belong to them."

"Well, they *did* decide to take back Alsace and Lorraine," Papa said, looking at the map. "But the paper says they aren't just going to occupy them; they are declaring them part of Germany. It will be terrible for the Jews there." He sighed and was silent for a while, studying the paper again.

Tears welled up in Maman's eyes. "Will people be able to get out of the occupied zone? Do you suppose there is any chance I could reach Geraldine again by telephone?"

Papa shook his head. "I'm sure that the Germans have cut off the phone connections between the two zones, as well as the mail and the telegraph service. There's no way to communicate." He looked at Gustave. "Why don't you go and play and meet us back at the house later," he said. "Maman and I need to talk."

"Be careful, Gustave," Maman added.

Gustave nodded and ran away from the tiny café. Did

they really think that he still didn't understand? Paris was a dangerous place to be now if you were Jewish. So was the whole occupied zone. The Nazis would rule that part of the country, would do whatever they wanted, to innocent people. But he wondered what the demarcation line between the two zones of France looked like. How could the Nazis make a line across a whole country? Would they paint a black line on the ground? Then why couldn't Jean-Paul's family or Marcel's or anyone who was trying to get out just run over the line when no one was looking?

Francueil was a quiet, empty-seeming little village, a lot like Saint-Georges. Gustave took his slingshot out of his back pocket and flicked a pebble ahead of him, watching it skitter up the road and stop at the top of the hill. He ran to pick it up. Just over the crest of another hill, three boys were kicking a soccer ball around the road. Two of them were about Gustave's age, and one was several years older. Gustave tucked his slingshot back into his pocket, studied their faces, then walked slowly forward. As he got closer, he heard the word "Boche." Everyone was talking about the Germans today.

"They won't get us," the tallest boy was saying, exultantly. "We're on the free side of the line."

The ball rolled toward Gustave, and he kicked it back to the boy nearest him, who had a friendly face.

"Are you new around here?" asked the boy.

"Yes," answered Gustave warily.

But the boy smiled and stretched out his hand. "I'm Henri. That's Julien"—he indicated the older boy—"and his brother, Luc."

81

Gustave and Henri shook hands. Julien stopped the ball under his right foot and looked at him.

"Have you seen the line?" Gustave asked them. "Is it on the ground?"

"Oh, it isn't a line on the ground," Henri said, but not as if Gustave were stupid for asking. "My uncle said that in some places, the Boches are putting up barbed wire. In other places, they march along and patrol it. Here, they use the river Cher for the line."

"They're putting up barriers at all the bridges," Julien explained. "Yesterday, we saw them building one near Saint-Georges. You want to go see?"

"Sure," said Gustave.

They kicked the ball back and forth all the way to the river.

"Do you go to school in Saint-Georges?" Gustave asked Henri on the way, feeling hopeful. It would be good to know someone friendly who might be in his class in the fall.

But Henri shook his head. "No, Luc and I both go to boarding school in Lyon. Look, there's the river." He picked up the ball and tucked it under his arm. Gathering into a tight group, the boys walked slowly forward.

At the bridge between Saint-Georges and Chissay, the village across the river, some German soldiers were installing a moving barrier on a post by the side of the road. One of them was painting a recently built shelter. When he smelled the wet paint, Gustave's feet moved more slowly. Would the Germans be able to tell that he was Jewish? If they could, what would they do? Maybe he should go back to the house. But he wanted to be with the other boys and see what was happening.

One of the soldiers looked up at the four boys and said something to the man next to him. They went on working. "Cowards," muttered Julien furiously. Gustave glanced up at Julien's scowling face. He had the dark shadow of a mustache on his upper lip. Henri murmured in agreement.

"Be quiet, Julien—they might hear you," said his younger brother nervously.

"I just can't stand them. Those filthy Boches!" said Julien, this time speaking loudly.

At that, the same soldier lifted his head again. He stood up, picked up his rifle, slung it over his shoulder, and strolled toward the boys, smiling slightly. As he got closer, Gustave could see that he was young, although his head was already nearly bald. He was short and slight, but he strutted as he walked, thrusting his chest out each time he took a step forward, like the rooster that lived behind Gustave's next-door neighbor's house.

"Do you have something to say to us, boys?" the German soldier asked. His French sounded foreign, harsh. Gustave wished he could run away, but his knees felt watery. No one said anything.

"Who said that word, 'Boche'?" The soldier wasn't smiling now. His eyes were cold and blue.

"I did," said Julien, stepping forward. He held his head high. He was taller than the German soldier.

"It is against the law to use that word now," said the soldier. "You know what we do to French people who say it?"

Julien didn't say anything.

"We shoot them," said the soldier smoothly.

He took his rifle down from his shoulder and pointed it at Julien's chest. Julien's face turned white. Luc gave a strangled cry. He started forward, but Henri grabbed his shirt and held him back.

But this is our side of the line! Gustave wanted to shout. You aren't in charge here! But his throat was choked, and he couldn't say anything. For a second, he couldn't swallow, couldn't breathe.

"At least, that's what we do to men," said the soldier. He was smiling broadly now, enjoying himself. "I guess we wouldn't do that to a little boy. Which are you?" he asked Julien. "A man or a little boy?"

Julien's face flooded with color. "I am sixteen," he said stiffly.

"So, you need to tell me," said the soldier. "If you tell me you are a man, I'll shoot you. If you say that you are a little boy, I won't. Which is it?"

There was a long pause as Julien stared at the soldier. Gustave felt his pulse pounding in his throat. The soldier shifted. Julien dropped his eyes.

"A boy," he muttered.

"I didn't quite hear that," said the German. His rifle clicked. "I'll give you one more chance. If you look at me and shout, 'I am a little boy,' I won't shoot you."

Julien looked up. His face was a furious crimson. "I am a little boy!" he shouted. His voice broke, and the last words squeaked out. The soldiers installing the barrier all looked up and laughed.

"Yes, you are," said the soldier. "Now you will march

here with me for an hour, up and down the bridge." He reached up, grabbed the back of Julien's neck, and squeezed, shoving his head down. Julien coughed, choking. The soldier squeezed Julien's neck again and shook it, his fingers digging into Julien's flesh. "You will shout out, over and over, 'This is a German, not a Boche. This is a German, not a Boche.'" He glared over at the other boys. "You—stand here and watch."

Julien marched with the soldier and shouted. Each time he came to the end of the bridge, the soldier shoved him to turn him around. Gustave and the others stood helplessly and watched. A streak of heat burned on each of Gustave's cheeks. How could he and the others let the soldier do that to Julien? His fingers moved to his back pocket. But what good was a slingshot? They were just kids. There was nothing they could do, and the soldier knew it. Gustave stood still and watched as the German had commanded them to, his body tingling with shame.

"Louder," said the soldier from time to time, smiling maliciously, glancing first at Julien and then at the younger boys. "Louder, boy."

Julien's eyes were glazed, his face now a dull purple-red. Long before the hour was up, he could no longer shout. His voice was a rasping whisper. The soldier finally let go of his neck, shoved him to the ground, and kicked him, twice. His boots thudded into Julien. Julien groaned. Gustave bit down on the tip of his tongue and clenched his fists. But he stood still, and so did Henri and Luc.

"Get away from here," the soldier said in disgust.

Julien scrambled to his feet. Without looking at anyone,

he stumbled away from the bridge and vomited on the side of the road. His younger brother ran after him, crying. Julien turned. "Leave me alone! Just leave me alone!" he croaked.

Luc continued to run, sobbing, away from the bridge, with Gustave and Henri right behind him. Without turning to say goodbye to Gustave, Henri and Luc ran off toward Francueil.

Before heading in the other direction, toward Saint-Georges, Gustave looked back. The balding German soldier was strolling over to join his comrades, whistling tunelessly, stopping to pick up stones and skip them into the river. The other soldiers had finished their carpentry while Julien was marching and shouting. The red-and-white-striped barrier rested on posts across the road over the bridge, dividing the two zones of France, its fresh paint gleaming in the morning sun.

When he got to the house, Gustave grabbed the folded newspaper off the kitchen table and ran upstairs. He snatched up his fountain pen, which was lying on the bureau. He looked at the demarcation line on the map in the newspaper, and he traced it furiously onto his map. It looked alien and ugly, curving up across the familiar shape of France. There was one more thing he had to do. He ran downstairs with his pitcher, pumped water into it in the kitchen, and raced back upstairs. The water sloshed out as he ran, but he didn't care. He scratched violently at the few bits of red paint left in the paint well and paused, breathing hard.

He ran his finger softly over the watercolor blue of Paris, where home was, where Marcel and Jean-Paul probably were still.

"Goodbye, Paris," he said, his voice hoarse.

Then he looked at the map in alarm. A dark smear of blood followed his finger, soaking into the paper. Gustave looked at his hand and breathed in sharply with surprise. The keen edge of the paint well had sliced the tip of his finger, and he hadn't even noticed. Now that he saw the wound, though, it started to throb painfully.

But he had to finish what he had started. He dripped water onto the last fragments of red and washed paint over the rest of the occupied zone, the watercolor pigment mingling with the dark stain on the map. Now the coast and the northern part of France were red too, just like all those other trampled countries. Blood-red. Gustave let out a gasping sob.

But the Nazis weren't supposed to bother people on this side of the line. He reached for the black pen again and wrote in all capital letters, below the line, *"ARRETEZ! ARRETEZ!"* He shouted the words as he wrote them. *STOP! STOP! STOP!*

Gustave jabbed the pen into the paper and traced the demarcation line over and over until the thin map ripped, startling him. It was a stupid map, anyway, almost all the same color. Smeared with red everywhere, it didn't separate anything from anything. Gustave grabbed it and tore it down from the wall, then ripped it into smaller and smaller pieces, until the floor was covered with the torn-up pieces of Europe.

12

Saint-Georges, September 1940

The night before school started in the fall, Gustave dreamed about Paris. A German soldier with a rifle slung over his shoulder had his hand clamped on Marcel's neck and was making him march down a long, dark street. When they were about to turn the corner, Marcel looked back at Gustave. In the moonlight, his face was white. Gustave tried to call out, but something choked his throat. He woke up making a strangled cry.

Gustave's mouth was too dry to swallow his bread at breakfast that morning. It didn't make him feel better when Maman sat down and looked earnestly at him across the table. "Remember, don't tell anyone at school that you're Jewish," she told him. "They might guess because of when we came from Paris, yet they may not if you say as little as you can about yourself. Becker is not an obviously Jewish last name."

"But can people tell we're Jewish by the way we look?" Gustave asked.

"Maybe," Maman said slowly. "You and Papa both have wavy, dark hair. But so do a lot of French people. No one could be *sure* you were Jewish just by looking."

"And, of course, you're circumcised—but no one is going to see that, right?" added Papa, smiling. "Just try to be inconspicuous," he went on. Gustave's hand was on the table, and Papa patted it. "Don't let anything bother you— try to get along with everybody so that you don't stand out."

Gustave nodded. But at school, the kids were sure to ask questions. How was he supposed to avoid answering? Gustave reached into his pocket, checking to make certain that Monkey was there. It would be embarrassing if anybody knew how often he carried Monkey around with him, but he didn't have any other friends in Saint-Georges.

The principal of Gustave's new school walked with him to his classroom and spoke in a hushed voice to the teacher, Monsieur Laroche. Monsieur Laroche had white hair and a weary face, but his voice was friendly.

"I would like you to meet Gustave Becker," he said to the class. "He comes to us from Paris. Let's go around the room and introduce ourselves." Gustave looked out at all the faces, some curious, some bored, as the names went by him in a blur. Then one face, in the back of the classroom, suddenly stood out. It was the pale-eyed boy who had shoved Gustave into the fountain. "Philippe," the boy said curtly when his turn came.

Gustave's heart pounded. Why did *that* kid have to be in his class? It was going to be hard not to get into any arguments with him around. Philippe's eyes bored into him. Gustave was glad when Monsieur Laroche handed him a book and pointed him to his desk.

At recess, a group of children gathered around Gustave.

"You're from Paris?" asked a girl. "Why did you come here?"

Philippe walked by the group and stopped. He pushed his lank, light hair away from his forehead, running his fingers through it. His hair looked greasy. "There are a lot of *youpins* in Paris, aren't there?" he called out.

Gustave's face burned, and the other kids looked at him curiously. Once, back in Paris, some boys had shouted *"Youpin!"*—*Yid!*—at Marcel. One had thrown a rock that cut Marcel's ear. Gustave didn't want to let the insulting word for Jews go by. But he wasn't supposed to let anyone guess that he was a Jew, so how could he defend Jews?

"Um, yeah," he said, looking at the ground. "I guess there are."

"I know what I'd do if I met a Yid," said a freckle-faced boy cheerfully. "My cousin met one once, and he baptized him. Problem solved! Not a Yid anymore!"

"How did he get the holy water?" a girl asked.

"Oh, you can use any kind," said the boy. He ran over to a puddle in the corner of the schoolyard, knelt down, and scooped up a handful of water in his cupped hands. "See, like this!" He smashed his clasped hands together and squirted the water at another boy through the space between his thumbs. "I baptize you, in the name of the Father, the Son, and the Holy Ghost!"

The wet boy yelled and knelt down to get a handful of water himself. Soon they were all running around the yard, shouting about the Holy Ghost.

Was it really true that the water could turn a Jew into a Catholic? Gustave's heart raced, and his palms felt clammy. What if someone did it to him? It was hard being Jewish, but it was who he was. He didn't want to become Catholic. The back of his neck felt very bare and exposed to the flying drops of water. Gustave turned and walked away stiffly, trying not to look as if he was hurrying.

In another part of the schoolyard, some kids were sitting on the ground. Gustave squatted near them, keeping his head down. Two boys and a girl in a blue dress with a white collar were trying to get three large, black beetles to race.

A little way apart, a girl with light brown curls was prodding at a cluster of beetles with a stick, pushing them into a line.

"Bring one over and race it with ours, Nicole!" called the girl in the blue dress.

"No, mine are soldiers," answered Nicole. She noticed Gustave watching her. "Look!" she said to him. She prodded the line of beetles with her stick. "March!" One of the beetles flew away, but the others moved obediently forward, still in the line. Their shiny backs looked like the boots of the Germans. Gustave's jaw clenched. He sprang to his feet and stamped, smashing the beetles that didn't scurry away quickly enough.

"Hey!" shouted Nicole, jumping up and shoving him. "What are you doing?"

"They look like the Boches!" Gustave panted.

"Oh." Nicole looked at him for a moment with her hands on her hips. "Well, they aren't. They're just beetles. Look." She sat back down and swept the insects together again with a stick.

She was right, of course. They were just beetles. Gustave sat down on the ground next to Nicole, his ears hot.

"How do you get them to line up and march?" he asked after a moment.

"Oh, just poke at them!" said the girl, grinning at him.

"One time my friend Marcel made a beetle spitball," said Gustave.

"Pas possible!" Nicole was scornful. "No way! I don't believe you. Your friend chewed up a beetle?"

"No, the beetle was attached to the spitball," Gustave explained. "Marcel tied one end of a piece of thread around a spitball and the other end around the middle of a beetle. He shot the spitball at the ceiling through a straw, and it stuck there. The beetle looked so funny, dangling there, wiggling its legs!"

"Ew!" said Nicole, giggling. "That's disgusting! But, honestly, it really worked?"

Gustave nodded, smiling. He and Marcel and Jean-Paul had all gotten into trouble that day for laughing in class, but none of them had told the teacher about the beetle, which stayed up there for at least an hour before falling down somewhere next to the teacher's desk and scurrying away.

"Do you happen to have any thread on you?" Nicole asked, her brown eyes gleaming. "Or maybe a piece of hair would work." She yanked one out of her head, then looked at it, disappointed. "But we don't have a straw to shoot the spitball with."

Just then a teacher rang the bell to call them in. Nicole waved and ran off to go in with her class, and Gustave lined up with his. None of the drops of baptismal water had landed on him, so he was still Jewish—even if it really was true that the water could have turned him Catholic. And Nicole was friendly and interesting.

But Nicole's class and his didn't usually have recess at the same time. Gustave looked around for her at recess for several days afterward before he figured that out. Claude, the freckle-faced boy whose cousin had baptized a Jew, was in Gustave's class, and he seemed friendly too, but he asked so many questions that Gustave wasn't supposed to answer.

"Why did you leave Paris?" Claude asked one day when he and Gustave were teamed up for a relay race.

"Because of the war," Gustave said. "My mother was worried about the bombs." That was partly true.

"So, are you going to go back now?" Claude persisted, panting, as he came back from running his leg of the race. "I wish I could go to Paris."

Gustave shrugged. "I don't know." Of course they weren't going back, so *that* really wasn't true. Claude didn't seem completely satisfied, but he let it go.

But one Monday morning, as Gustave slid into his seat, Claude looked over at him and asked, curiously, "How come I never see you at church?"

Philippe sat on the other side of Claude. "Yeah, why not, Paris boy?" he sneered.

Gustave froze. He couldn't think of a single excuse, and his tongue wouldn't move, anyway. He heard his watch ticking, slowly. He opened his mouth, about to mumble something—he didn't know what, maybe something about Papa's limp and the long walk—when Monsieur Laroche rang the bell to signal the beginning of class. Gustave's breathing slowly went back to normal.

But how could he make friends when he couldn't tell the truth? With Philippe around, always butting in, making friends was just about impossible, anyway. Gustave's thoughts whirled while Monsieur Laroche talked about grammar. Why did Philippe act like that? What if someone did find out for sure that Gustave's family was Jewish? Could that be a problem even here, in the unoccupied zone? What did Maman and Papa think would happen here in Saint-Georges if people knew?

13

Gustave's parents were having problems too.

"*Incroyable!*" Papa shouted, shaking the newspaper one morning in October. He banged on the table, making the dishes rattle and almost spilling his cup of coffee. "Unbelievable! How can our own government do such a thing? It's an outrage!" He read aloud from the paper. " 'Jews are forbidden to hold jobs in government, the law, and civil service. All Jewish teachers will be fired from the public schools. Jews may no longer work in radio or in film or as newspaper reporters or editors.' "

"These are French laws, laws from our own government?" Maman asked, twisting a dish towel between her hands. "Not laws from the Germans?"

"Not *our* government, Lili!" Papa exploded. "The new France with *Vichy* laws. I tell you, Maréchal Pétain and the

95

Vichy government are worse than useless. And I closed up the store in Paris just in the nick of time. If we still lived there, it would have been taken away from us. The Germans are taking over all Jewish-owned businesses. What is happening to our country?"

Pétain's picture hung on the wall of every classroom in the school. Gustave usually tried to avoid looking at the stern old face with its bushy white mustache, but that morning he stared at it after he finished his page of math exercises, as if somehow the face could make him understand. Why would a Frenchman, a military hero, make so many Jews lose their jobs? How could people live if they couldn't work?

Maman was upset every evening when the mailbox was empty. The Germans had finally decided to let mail cross the demarcation line between the two zones of France, but you could send only preprinted postcards with messages to circle or cross out, saying things like "We are well" or "We are ill." Maman bought one in the village, circled a few messages, and sent it to Aunt Geraldine. But the Nazis let only a few of the cards go across every day, and people were saying that many were getting lost or thrown away at the border. No cards had come yet from Paris, nothing from Aunt Geraldine or from Marcel's mother, Madame Landau.

One evening, as the weather was getting cooler, Gustave saw that Maman had tears in her eyes as she ladled soup into bowls at dinner. "There's just no food here," she said. "How am I supposed to make a meal with yesterday's bread and rutabagas? That's all I could buy today. The shopkeepers say that the government takes all the food directly from the farmers to give to the Germans. The only reason I can get rutabagas is because the Germans don't like them."

"We have nothing more in the garden?" asked Papa.

Gustave scooped up a spoonful of stringy mashed rutabagas, stuck it into his mouth, and quickly gulped water so that he could swallow without tasting it. He hated rutabagas too, but they filled his stomach.

"All that work for nothing," Gustave said. Practically every day all summer, Maman had made him weed that garden.

"Well, not for nothing," said Maman. "We harvested those tomatoes and green beans. But I wish we had gotten just a few radishes. Those would have kept over the winter, and they would have made the bread taste more interesting. But I think those seeds were no good. They just didn't grow. Or maybe something ate them." She sighed.

Gustave bit into his stale bread, imagining how much better it would taste with creamy butter and the spicy tingle of black radish. He and Maman both loved those radishes. So did Aunt Geraldine. One day last fall in Paris, Gustave, Jean-Paul, and Marcel had been the first to see that black radishes were for sale in the outdoor market and that people were lining up to buy them. The three of them had waited in line for ten minutes to buy some. Their mothers had been delighted when they'd come home. Gustave's family had invited Jean-Paul's and Marcel's over for lunch, and they had shared the first gnarled, twisty black radishes, peeled and sliced very, very thin, on buttered chunks of bread.

"How thick a piece of radish can you eat just plain?" Marcel had asked Jean-Paul, cutting himself a slice twice as thick as usual, biting into it, then quickly swallowing water. Jean-Paul had sliced one as thick as his thumb. He held the radish piece in front of his mouth for a moment, grinning at Gustave and Marcel, before taking a huge bite. The other boys had watched, fascinated, as Jean-Paul's face slowly flushed a deep scarlet.

"Ah!" he screamed, running for the bathroom to spit it out.

"Boys, please don't waste food," Maman had said pleasantly as Jean-Paul gulped down almost the whole pitcher of water to cool his tongue. She wouldn't say that so calmly now, Gustave thought. The chunk of radish Jean-Paul had spat out that day last fall would have been enough to flavor his bread and Maman's and Papa's for several meals.

"Some of the farmers *must* have hidden food away from the Germans," Papa said, gripping the table so vigorously that Gustave's spoon fell out of his soup. "And I have all that leftover stock from the store. It's time to start making use of it. People need shoes and cloth as much now as ever, and there's nothing in the stores."

"Oh, Berthold, be careful," Maman whispered.

Papa lowered his voice. "Wait and see. Tomorrow maybe I'll be able to find a farmer who will trade a nice, plump chicken for a pair of good leather shoes."

Maman anxiously twisted her napkin between her fingers. "That's the black market, Berthold," she whispered again. "You know that the government has declared that sort of trading illegal."

"As a Jew, I can't run my business now," Papa said fiercely. "And I'm certainly not going to let good leather shoes rot while we starve."

Dinner the next night was much more filling. Papa came home with a whole sack of potatoes and three eggs that a farmer had given him in exchange for two pairs of children's shoes. Maman made hot, crispy potato pancakes. A week later, Papa came home with something even better.

"Look what I have today!" he said to Maman, kissing her on the cheek. "A whole kilo of butter and a bag of apples! I traded the farmer for a pair of slippers."

Maman made a rich, buttery apple tart that night, and for the next several weeks, the food was better. But after the first frost, Papa came home with less and less.

Then one day, Gustave was sitting on the living room floor, working on a jigsaw puzzle picturing the Arc de Triomphe in Paris, when Papa bounded in, beaming.

"Voilà!" he said. "Look what I have for us tonight!" He pulled a plucked chicken out of his sack.

"Chicken!" Gustave's stomach rumbled. They hadn't eaten meat in months. "Where did you get it?" he asked joyfully, jumping up from the floor to get a better look. "I can't believe it, Papa!"

But Maman was frowning in the doorway. "Where *did* you get it, Berthold?" she asked, with an edge to her voice.

Gustave glanced from one of his parents to the other. Why was Maman upset? He ducked back down to the floor and flipped over puzzle pieces, looking for a corner. He only needed to find the fourth corner piece to complete the frame.

"It comes from just over the river," Papa replied calmly. "The farmers on our side of the Cher mostly cultivate grapes for wine. But what we need is food. There's more at the farms on the other side of the demarcation line."

"You crossed over the line into the occupied zone?" Maman's voice was high and thin. "What if the Nazis had given you trouble?"

"I'm not going to let the Germans stop me from crossing a French river," said Papa evenly. "I used my Swiss identity papers. I tell you, the farmers and the men I meet at the cafés envy me for having Swiss papers and being able to cross the line."

Maman sighed. "I don't like it. It isn't safe."

"We have to eat, Lili," said Papa, throwing himself into one of the armchairs. Maman sighed again and went into the kitchen.

When she was out of the room, Gustave fit another piece into his puzzle and looked up at his father. "Why is it good to have Swiss papers?" he asked quietly.

"You know how the Germans are letting some French people cross the line now?" Papa answered. "You can apply to them for a pass to cross the line, but I hear it is a big runaround to get one. But with Swiss papers, I don't need a pass. I can cross anytime, since Switzerland is a neutral country, not fighting in the war."

Gustave ran his finger over the edge of a puzzle piece. "But then why can't Jean-Paul's family and Marcel's just get passes and leave the occupied zone?" he asked.

Papa leaned back, and the armchair creaked. "The Nazi

officials give those passes to a few of the French people who apply for them," he said. "But not to Jews. They won't do any favors for Jews."

Soon the house was filled with the delicious smell of roasting chicken. But everyone was quiet at dinner. Gustave chewed the rich, tender meat, watching his parents. Finally, Maman said, "You're right that we need to eat, Berthold. But please be careful. And next time, I'll write a letter to Geraldine, and you can mail it from the other side of the line. Even though that's illegal too. But that way, there's more of a chance she'll get our letter, even if we can't hear back from her."

Papa smiled, rubbing her arm. "Don't worry," he said. "The Germans want to stay on the good side of the Swiss government. The guards at the line won't bother me. I'll only go if we really need the food."

So every now and then, Papa bounded into the house with something special—a full dozen eggs, a bunch of carrots, or a wheel of cheese. One night, Maman slit open the seam of a cloth bag, tucked in a letter to Aunt Geraldine, and sewed it neatly closed. Papa took the letter across to mail it. On the days when he came back from his bartering trips with something particularly good, he acted the way he used to in Paris when he had had an especially good day at the store: he kissed Maman and whistled around the house, and sometimes he played with Gustave after dinner. One cool fall evening, Papa even pulled himself up the ladder in the garage to admire Gustave's fort.

* * *

The road in front of the school was full of exuberant children on the last Thursday in October, the day before La Toussaint. As Gustave made his way around a group of girls with their arms linked, who were singing at the top of their lungs, Claude ran toward him.

"Think fast!" He threw a pinecone at Gustave's head.

"Hey!" Gustave picked it up and threw it back.

Nicole and a girl named Celeste, who was always playing hopscotch at recess, broke away from the group of singing girls and joined him and Claude. The four of them started toward home.

"No homework for a week!" Celeste said gleefully, tossing her blond head and glancing at Gustave with vivid blue eyes.

"Do your families have food for the All Souls' supper?" Claude asked the others. "Are you having bacon? We don't have any left, so we're just having pancakes, cider, and pears. But bacon is the best part!"

"We have some," Celeste said. "My mother's been saving it. But we have eight people coming, so there won't be much for each. Do you have any? Or any *rillettes*?" She looked straight at Gustave.

Gustave's throat tightened with disgust at the thought. Bacon or *rillettes*? Of course not. Both were made from pork, and Jews didn't eat pork. La Toussaint was a Catholic holiday, and none of the kids from his neighborhood in Paris celebrated it. He didn't even really know what Catholics did on La Toussaint, just that for everybody, it was the beginning of a week off from school. But he couldn't say that. Nervously, he shoved his hands into his pockets, frantically trying to think of something to say.

"Wake up, Gustave!" Claude knocked on his head. "Anybody in there? Celeste asked if your family has bacon for the All Souls' supper."

"We don't!" Nicole jumped in. "I'm just glad that we have enough eggs for pancakes. I like the cider and hazelnuts and pancakes best, anyway. Oh, and I really love the roasted *marrons*. I always smell those chestnuts that Monsieur Arnaud sells outside the cemetery when we're saying the prayers over the graves. Once, my father let me buy some when we came out, but when my aunt comes to visit, she tells my father not to spoil my appetite. As if it would! My aunt is so annoying! When she and my uncle and cousins visit, she always tells my father that I'm a hooligan and that he isn't raising me properly. She never likes the dresses I wear when we go to decorate my mother's grave. Anyway, could you buy a pot of chrysanthemums to decorate the graves with? We couldn't, but I know where some purple aster is growing. I think it's pretty, and my mother loved wildflowers, but my aunt will never approve. She doesn't even approve of colored chrysanthemums for my mother's grave, only white. . . ." Nicole went on and on, hardly stopping to take a breath.

Startled, Gustave looked at her. Nicole sure could talk. And she didn't have a mother? Gustave hadn't realized that.

Celeste put her arm around Nicole's waist. "I'm sorry," she said when Nicole paused. "For a minute I forgot about your mother. It must be a hard holiday for you."

"I miss her when I think about her," Nicole said, more quietly. "But I was so little, only three, when she died. But my aunt," she continued, more cheerfully, "you should hear her going on about my hair, and my table manners, and the people Papa associates with, and my bicycle riding, and my bedtime. . . ."

Nicole chattered on and on until Claude came to his turnoff. Then Celeste, hiding her face behind a curtain of blond hair, tugged Nicole's arm insistently, and the two of them ran off, saying that they were going to the *boulangerie*.

"Goodbye, Gustave!" Celeste called over her shoulder, giggling.

Gustave nodded and headed toward his house, wondering what Celeste was giggling about. Nicole seemed a lot more sensible. It must be hard for Nicole, not having a mother. But he was glad that she had talked so much after Celeste had asked about bacon and *rillettes*. It almost seemed as if Nicole had deliberately chattered so much so that he wouldn't have to answer.

But then that must mean that Nicole suspected he wasn't Catholic, Gustave thought nervously. Why had she noticed when the others hadn't? Did that mean that she realized he was Jewish? But if she did, why was she helping him hide it?

14

The first few days of the La Toussaint school holiday were sunny, but then the weather turned bitterly cold. On Wednesday morning, after Maman left for work, Gustave was huddled on his bed, wearing his warmest sweater with the wool blanket over him, rereading *The Three Musketeers* for the hundredth time, when Papa came in.

"I have an adventure for us," Papa said, smiling.

Gustave jumped up from the bed. "What are we going to do?"

"We're going bartering," Papa said. "A farmer yesterday told me about another farm where they have ducks and need woolen cloth. It's about thirty kilometers away, and he offered me a can of gasoline in our exchange yesterday, so this time we can take the truck."

Gustave helped Papa heave a heavy roll of woolen cloth into the back of the truck.

"No one will notice that cloth unless they're really looking!" Papa exclaimed as he threw a sheet of canvas over it. "Not that the Germans really care what you bring *into* the occupied zone. But if they see something they want, they'll find an excuse to confiscate it."

"We're going into the occupied zone?" Gustave shivered and tucked his hands under his armpits to warm them.

"None of the farms on this side have any meat to spare," Papa said. "Or much food of any kind, now that it's winter." He picked up a heavy box and shoved it into the truck, positioning it in front of the roll of cloth. "That's why I need you to come along," he went on, straightening up. "I don't want them to search the truck when we cross the demarcation line coming back. They do search every now and then, but I've never seen them do that when there's a child in the vehicle. A man alone is a more suspicious character, I guess."

"But I'm not Swiss," Gustave said. "Don't I need a pass?" He handed Papa another box.

Papa slid it into the truck. "My papers will do for us both," he answered. "Don't worry."

"Where are we going to cross the river?" Gustave asked, blowing on his fingers and trying to sound curious, not nervous. "At the bridge between Saint-Georges and Chissay?" Even with Papa, he didn't want to cross over the bridge where Julien had marched.

"No, at Montrichard," Papa answered. "I've gotten to know Hans, one of the guards at the border there. Since

106

it's Wednesday, he'll be on duty. It helps to have the right papers, but it also doesn't hurt that I learned German growing up in Switzerland, so I can joke around with him in his native language." Papa laughed as he slammed the rear of the truck closed. "If I ask him about his girlfriend on our return trip, we'll *really* hold up the traffic behind us! He'll be much too busy telling me how much he misses her to look for black-market food." Papa started to whistle as they climbed into the truck.

They wound through the roads heading toward the Montrichard bridge. The sheen of ice glittered on the river. As they got to the line at the checkpoint, Papa stopped whistling and slowed the truck, stopping behind a shiny, black automobile. Gustave peered ahead. A striped barrier blocked the road, with a guards' shelter behind it. A red German flag with a black swastika waved in the French wind. Gustave winced. Below, a sign had words in dark Gothic type: DEMARKATIONSLINIE. *Demarcation Line.* You didn't need to understand German to know what that meant.

Papa looked over at Gustave, his face suddenly grave.

"But I hear they have started watching the line more carefully lately," he said. "When we come to the checkpoint, don't say anything. Let me do the talking."

15

As the car ahead of Papa's truck moved forward, a stocky, blond German soldier strode toward Papa's truck, holding his hand up. "Halt!" he barked. The morning light glinted on the rifle strapped over his shoulder.

Papa drew his breath in sharply. "Who is that?" he muttered under his breath. "Not Hans."

The soldier peered in through Papa's window. "Out! Out of the truck!" he commanded in harsh, heavily accented French. Papa opened the door and stepped down. The soldier's face loomed through the windshield at Gustave. "You!" he shouted. "I said out! Right now!"

Gustave's fingers were so stiff and shaky that he could hardly push the door open. When he finally did, he tripped over a loose shoelace and almost fell as he hurried to Papa. The two stood shoulder to shoulder, their breath making clouds in the air. The soldier leaned into the cab of the truck and looked under the seats. Then he walked around and opened the rear door. After a few minutes, he came back toward them.

"Your papers!" he demanded, stretching out a black-gloved hand.

Papa reached inside his coat and handed the papers to the soldier. He said something in German, his voice friendly and respectful. The soldier started and looked directly into Papa's eyes for the first time. Papa spoke again, and the soldier answered in German, his voice more steady than before. Gustave listened intently. He could understand a few words his father said—*"Guten Morgen, Herr Offizier,"* and *"Schweiz,"* *Good morning, Officer,* and *Switzerland*—but the other words were a meaningless blur of sound.

The soldier examined the papers again, then said something to Papa. He turned, still holding the papers, and walked back toward the shelter.

The wind gusted, hitting Gustave's face like a slap. He shoved his hands as deeply as he could into his pockets, closing his left hand around Monkey's warm fur. He was wearing last year's too-small coat. The sleeves didn't reach as far as his wrists, and the pockets felt too high. His bare wrists were freezing. The harsh wind lifted bits of dust that stung his eyes. Gustave stamped his feet, trying to keep warm. He looked across the river and watched the wind swaying the bare branches of the tall poplar trees.

It seemed a long time before the soldier stepped out of the shelter. Gustave watched his father prepare his face in a genial smile as the soldier walked toward them.

When the German spoke to Papa, his voice sounded less stern. Gustave heard the word *"Schweiz"* again. The soldier handed the papers back, and Papa stowed them carefully away inside the inner pocket of his coat. The soldier lifted the striped barrier, and Papa drove over the bridge.

"What happened?" Gustave asked when they were out of sight of the guard. "What was wrong? Why did we have to get out?"

"He was suspicious," said Papa. "I'm not sure why. Maybe he's just suspicious of everybody, or maybe he·thought we looked Jewish and wanted to give us trouble. He didn't know we were Swiss citizens until he looked at my papers."

With a sudden pang, Gustave remembered the swaying men and the chanting voices in the synagogue where they used to go in Paris. Here in Saint-Georges, they had celebrated the Jewish High Holidays at home, quietly, just the three of them, dipping apples in honey at the dinner table on Rosh Hashanah and fasting and praying at home, with the shutters tightly fastened, on Yom Kippur. But in Paris they always went to the synagogue. When Gustave was smaller, after he had been on the main floor with Papa and the men for a while, he would run down the aisle to play in the lobby with Jean-Paul and Marcel. Sometimes the three of them climbed upstairs to the women's gallery. Gustave liked to lean over the railing and look down at the tops of the men's dark hats. He could always pick out Papa's because it had a dent in the front.

One day, winking at Gustave and Jean-Paul, Marcel had stretched out his hand and quickly scattered a fistful of hazelnuts over the railing. One landed right on someone's prayer book. A young man with glasses and a light brown beard looked up, bewildered, as if he thought something had fallen from heaven. Jean-Paul, Marcel, and Gustave had had such a fit of laughter that the women had scolded them and sent them downstairs. Marcel swore to his mother, over and over, that he had dropped it accidentally.

"Accidentally on purpose," he had admitted later, laughing, to Jean-Paul and Gustave.

"I'm glad I look Jewish," Gustave said fiercely now to Papa, surprising himself. "I'm proud that I'm a Jew." Suddenly, Gustave remembered that first day in the schoolyard when he had agreed with Philippe that there were a lot of Yids in Paris, and a wave of shame washed over him. He turned his head away, leaning his forehead against the cold glass of the window. But what else could he have done? At least he hadn't let anyone baptize him that day when he thought it might turn him into a Catholic.

"Yes, of course," said Papa. "But these are dangerous times for Jews."

Especially here in the occupied zone, Gustave thought. If only Papa could just keep driving all the way to Paris, pick up Jean-Paul's family and the Landaus, and bring them all back to Saint-Georges, where it was safer. But it was impossible to get that much gasoline. And Jean-Paul's family and Marcel's couldn't cross the demarcation line without the proper papers. Especially not with guards like that one in charge.

"Why was there a different German soldier at the checkpoint, anyway?" Gustave asked. "When will Hans be back?"

"Hans is gone. Transferred to another post." Papa let out a sudden short, hard laugh. "But just watch. I'll get this soldier to be friendly with me too."

Gustave rubbed his hands nervously against his legs to warm them. Sure, Papa was funny, and he spoke German fluently. But could even his father make a man like that soldier today joke with him the way he said that Hans used to? That soldier, with the hard face and barking voice? And later today they would be coming back home, crossing the line the other way, with ducks hidden in the back of the truck. Ducks bought on the black market. Ducks that the new German law said that they were not allowed to buy.

Papa said that he had made a good hiding place in the truck. But what if the German guards searched it? If that was what it was like going in, what would it be like trying to come out? Did Papa know that the Germans shot people just for saying the word "Boche"? Gustave wondered. He remembered the rifle aimed at Julien's chest and flushed again with the humiliation and helplessness of that day. If the German soldiers could do that just because of a word, what would they do if they caught Papa and Gustave with black-market ducks? Although it was warmer in the cab of the truck than it had been outside, Gustave shivered again and pulled his too-small coat tightly around himself.

16

The small villages in the occupied zone looked a lot like the villages on the south side of the Cher except that the clock on a church read three o'clock when it should have been two.

"It's an hour ahead here," Papa explained. "The Germans set the time forward to accord with German time."

As they drove through one town, Gustave saw a long, red Nazi banner with a black swastika in a white circle draped over the whole front of the *mairie,* the town hall. In the square in the town center, German soldiers in uniform lounged on the benches, laughing and smoking. The French street signs had been replaced with German ones. Gustave angrily bit the tip of his tongue. They acted as if they owned France. Was that what it was like in Paris now? Did Marcel and Jean-Paul have to see soldiers like that every day? Gustave was glad when he and his father were out among the fields again.

As they pulled up to the farm where Papa had heard there would be ducks, Gustave wound his watch forward one hour so that he would know what time it was. He and Papa stepped down from the truck as two women came out of the house. Both were tall and strongly built. The older one had short, white hair, and the younger carried a little girl in her arms. The young woman set the child down, and the girl squatted on the ground to play while the older woman watched. The young woman came toward the truck.

Papa stretched his hand out to her. "Friends suggested that we should meet," he said, smiling.

The younger woman smiled back, shaking Papa's hand. "You're the man with the Swiss papers?" she asked.

" 'Tain! 'Tain!" shrieked the little girl suddenly.

Her mother turned around, startled.

"Marie!" shouted the grandmother, waving something toward the young woman and Papa. "You told me you had gotten rid of this dreadful doll!" She took several nimble steps toward an old cistern, wrenched off the top, and tossed something in.

The little girl wailed.

Marie ran to pick up the crying child. "Look what you have done, Mère Hélène!" she exclaimed. "Marguerite is just a baby, and it was just a piece of knitting! Couldn't you have simply cut off the *képi*, the military cap, and the little white mustache?"

The grandmother walked back, her cheeks pink.

114

"I just couldn't stand seeing my granddaughter cuddling a Maréchal Pétain doll. I would always have known it was him, in his little khaki uniform. Why did you let that nun give it to her?" She shrugged, looking a little embarrassed. "Well, what's done is done. I didn't mean to upset the little one." Marguerite continued to cry. Her grandmother patted her awkwardly, but Marguerite hid her face against her mother's shoulder.

"I apologize for the uproar." The younger woman turned back to Papa. "I am Marie Robert, and this is my mother-in-law, Madame Hélène Robert."

Papa shook hands with them both. "Berthold," he said. "And this is my son, Gustave. And I agree with you about Pétain, Madame Robert," he added.

The older woman's cheeks flushed once more. "When is he going to bring our soldiers home?" she exclaimed. "How could he let the Boches make them all prisoners of war? France is losing all dignity." She stopped and looked steadily at Papa for a moment. "And the restrictions against the Jews," she added, more quietly. "Completely immoral."

Papa nodded slowly. The two of them held each other's gaze. Then the grandmother turned to the younger Madame Robert. "I will show Berthold the ducks, Marie," she said. "Why don't you take Marguerite and Gustave into the kitchen, where it's warm. We'll be back in a few minutes."

Inside the kitchen, Marguerite, who had stopped wailing, squirmed, and her mother put her down. She toddled right toward Gustave and grabbed his leg. Gustave looked down. She was reaching for Monkey, who was peeking out of his pocket. He pulled out the small stuffed animal and wiggled him for her. The baby laughed in a funny, bubbly way that reminded Gustave, with a sudden pang, of Jean-Paul's baby sister, Giselle. She had wisps of curling light brown hair too, a lot like Giselle's. Gustave gently put his finger through one of the curls. It was soft and light, like down. When Marguerite tugged on Monkey again, Gustave let her hold him. Inside, she couldn't drop him in the dirt.

"Oh, that's nice of you, Gustave!" said Madame Robert as she opened a drawer and pulled out a paring knife. She stood chopping carrots and onions at a scarred wooden kitchen table. "What with this war, we can't find any toys to buy for her. That Maréchal Pétain doll was her only toy, but I understand why my mother-in-law couldn't stand it."

The older Madame Robert came in with Papa, letting a gust of cold air into the kitchen. "A good deal for both of us," she said contentedly. "We have enough soup to invite Berthold and his son to eat with us, don't we, Marie?" she said, tapping the younger woman on the shoulder.

"Thank you!" said Papa. "You're very generous."

At the table, Gustave spooned up his soup hungrily, listening to the adults talk about living in the occupied zone. The soup had lots of different vegetables in it, not just rutabagas. It was delicious.

"Here we have to hide the animals and the produce from the Boches," the older Madame Robert complained. "If not, they drive right up in their trucks and take it all, paying about one-tenth of what it's worth. But they're stupid," she added, smiling. "We can keep a lot hidden."

"And I can't get a pass to get across the line to see my mother," the younger Madame Robert said. "My mother hasn't seen Marguerite since before she could walk."

"Imagine keeping a grandmother from seeing her granddaughter," added her mother-in-law. "No feeling, those Germans." She reached out and gently stroked Marguerite's head with gnarled fingers as the little girl sat playing with Monkey on the floor by the table.

"Where does your mother live? I could stop in and tell her how you are doing," Papa offered.

"Would you?" The young woman beamed, and she went through a long list of things for Papa to tell her mother when he saw her.

"So, you say you have winter boots that would fit Marguerite?" said the grandmother when the meal was over. "Can you bring them soon?"

"Absolutely," said Papa. "Next week?"

Gustave went over to Marguerite. "I need Monkey back," he said. "We're going home."

Marguerite scrambled to her feet, clutching Monkey tightly, and burst into tears.

The grown-ups all looked over. Gustave's cheeks burned. Marguerite didn't have any other dolls or toys. He felt sorry for her. It would be hard to see your doll drowned in the cistern, even if it *was* a Pétain doll. But Monkey was his.

"Marguerite," said her mother sternly. "The monkey belongs to Gustave. Be a good girl and give him back."

Marguerite just wept more loudly.

Out of the corner of his eye, Gustave saw Papa glance at him. Papa had been hinting lately that maybe Gustave

117

was too old to carry Monkey around in his pocket so much. "I guess Marguerite can borrow him until next week," Gustave said slowly. "Until my father brings the boots."

"Well, if you are really sure?" said the younger Madame Robert. "So, Marguerite, you can play with Monkey for a few days. But when Gustave's father comes back, we'll give Monkey back to him."

Marguerite immediately stopped crying and hugged Gustave. Gustave patted the wooly brown fur on Monkey's head. He wasn't a little kid anymore. He didn't need to have Monkey with him all the time. But for some reason, his throat hurt.

The older Madame Robert was watching him. "May we give the boy a little something to thank him, Berthold?" she said to Papa. She stepped up on a chair, opening a high cupboard in the kitchen, and brought down something wrapped in silver paper.

"Half a bar of Swiss chocolate!" she said. "We've been saving it since before the war."

Gustave smelled the richness of chocolate, but he shook his head, looking back at Marguerite and Monkey. "No, thank you," he said.

"No?" said the grandmother. "Is there something else you would like from the farm?"

Gustave hesitated. But the grandmother seemed to want to give him something.

"In the summer, did you grow any black radishes?" he asked.

"Radishes!" Madame Robert laughed. "A boy who likes radishes better than chocolate?"

Papa smiled over at Gustave. "Oh, his mother especially loves those radishes," he said. "Gustave does too."

"I think there are a few left in the cellar," said the grandmother. "I'll go see." She brought up two long, twisty black radishes, almost as long as Gustave's forearm, and handed them to him. *"Bon appétit!"* she said. "I hope you and your family enjoy them."

The younger Madame Robert came out of the farmhouse, carrying Marguerite, as Gustave and his father got into the truck. Marguerite clutched Monkey and waved goodbye. Gustave looked back as they drove away, watching the tall woman with the little girl perched high in her arms getting smaller and smaller. As they went farther down the road, he couldn't see the speck that was Monkey anymore, and then he could no longer see Madame Robert and Marguerite.

"What a nice family," Papa said. "I'll go back another day next week with the little boots."

"The soup was good too."

"They have more food on the farms. As they say, you can't drown a sailor and you can't starve a farmer," Papa answered.

"Maman is going to be so happy about these," Gustave said, running his hand over the two dark, gnarled radishes on his lap. Maybe Gustave couldn't transport his friends and their families across the demarcation line—not without the right papers—but at least he could bring his mother her favorite radishes.

17

It was five-forty p.m. on Gustave's watch and getting dark and bitterly cold when they arrived at the demarcation line. There was a car with a spare tire on its roof up ahead, and several men stood, shivering and stamping their feet, holding bicycles, in the line just in front of them. Papa turned off the engine to wait. Things seemed to be moving very slowly. Gustave watched his father's fingers gripping the steering wheel. Coming back across the line, Papa always tried to arrive just at the end of the guards' shift, when they were tired and less likely to be thorough. But arriving at this hour was risky, because it was hard to time it just right. When the day shift ended, at six o'clock, the new guards came on, well rested and in no hurry.

The car with the spare tire moved forward across the

line, and two of the soldiers walked over to the men with bicycles. Gustave recognized one of them as the stocky blond soldier who had made them get out of the truck earlier in the day. The blond soldier said something to one of the Frenchmen with bicycles, and the Frenchman unbuttoned his coat and took it off. The blond German shook out the coat, then slowly reached inside all the pockets, turning them inside out. When he had finished examining the coat, the soldier dropped it onto the road. One of the sleeves landed in an icy puddle. The Frenchman leaned down to pick it up. But as he reached for it, the German, grinning, slammed his boot down, hard, on top of the coat, just missing the man's fingers. The man straightened, shivering, and crossed his arms against his chest.

Gustave looked at Papa. He was watching too, his face grim. After asking a lot of questions, the blond soldier finally moved his boot and kicked the coat toward the Frenchman. The man picked up his coat, hastily brushed it off, squeezed out the wet sleeve, and put it on. He blew on his fingers and buttoned the coat rapidly, then swung his leg over the bicycle and pedaled off. Now there were only two men on bicycles ahead. Another car pulled up behind them and came to a stop.

The soldier Gustave did not recognize walked back toward the truck, and Papa rolled down the window. He was older than the burly, blond German, and he had curly reddish brown hair and a wide, snub-nosed face. Gustave relaxed his hands, suddenly realizing that he had been clenching them in his lap.

"*Bonsoir,*" said the German, in foreign-sounding French.

"*Guten Abend, Herr Offizier,*" Papa said in German, smiling politely and handing him the papers. Gustave could understand those words—"*Good evening, Officer*"—but not the other German words that followed. The snub-nosed soldier chuckled at something and nodded. Then the big, blond soldier, who was still examining the papers of one of the men on bicycles, looked back over his shoulder and shouted something. The soldier by the truck stopped smiling and walked back to the larger man.

"What did he say, Papa?" whispered Gustave.

"He said to search the truck," Papa answered very quietly. "Don't worry. The ducks are well hidden."

But Papa's smile, when he turned toward the returning soldier, didn't look real. And although he was making his voice sound cheerful, Gustave could hear the tension underneath. Just then, someone banged on Gustave's window, and he jumped. It was a third soldier, with thick, greasy-looking dark eyebrows. Gustave rolled down the window, his hand shaking.

The soldier looked at the watch on Gustave's wrist, then spoke in French. "What time is it?" he asked.

Gustave held up his watch so that the man could see.

"Five fifty-five! You are on German time, I see. Good boy! What have you got there?"

The soldier reached for one of the radishes and picked it up by the stalk. "Ah! Black radishes! Nice big ones. Georg!" he called to the blond soldier. "Come see! Beer radishes!"

The burly blond soldier walked over to Gustave's side of the truck, grinning, his rifle swinging as he walked. Gustave's heart thudded. He folded his arms over the remaining radish on his lap, but there was no way to hide it now. The soldier with the black eyebrows dangled the first radish up high by its stalk, said something in German, and laughed uproariously. The massive blond soldier chuckled, grabbing at the dangling radish with a beefy hand. They spoke to one another in German, and the blond soldier slapped the one with black eyebrows on the back.

Then both of their faces came up close to the open window. Gustave leaned back, trying to get away from their sour breath. The soldier with the black eyebrows spoke. "What does a boy like you need beer radishes for? Are you planning on drinking tonight?" He laughed loudly, and a gold filling glinted in his mouth.

Gustave knew what he had to do. The Germans wanted the radishes. Somewhere in the truck, his father had hidden the black-market ducks. If the Germans searched the truck, they might find them. Gustave slowly picked up the other radish on his lap. Cradling it in both hands for a moment, he passed it out the window.

"Ah, very nice! Too bad you aren't a little older so that you could come drink with us." The soldier with the black eyebrows smirked and banged a triumphant rat-a-tat-tat on the side of the truck again. The burly blond soldier, laughing now, said something to the first soldier who had spoken to Papa, who was still standing on Papa's side of the truck. That soldier walked to the back of the vehicle, opened it, glanced in, and slammed the door closed. He walked back to Papa's window, said something, gestured Papa forward, and raised the striped barrier.

Gustave's blood pounded in his head as they drove on, and his fingers trembled. What right did the German soldiers have to take his radishes? What *right*?

"Why did they call them beer radishes, Papa?" he burst out when they had driven several kilometers and the demarcation line was far behind them.

"Germans slice up radishes and salt them to dry them out," said Papa grimly. "Then they eat them while they drink beer. They must be planning quite a party."

"What a stupid thing to do with radishes," Gustave exploded.

"I'm really sorry that happened, Gustave," Papa said after a while. "I didn't think they would bother about vegetables. But you were smart to give them the second radish. It stopped them from searching the truck."

"But now I can't bring the radishes to Maman," Gustave said. His voice wavered, and he bit down on his lip. He looked out the truck window into the darkness beyond it, and without thinking about what he was doing, he reached into his coat pocket to rub Monkey's head. But Monkey wasn't there. He was in the occupied zone, divided from Gustave by the demarcation line. Those soldiers with the big, laughing mouths and the cold eyes stood guard between Gustave and Monkey—and also between him and Jean-Paul and Marcel. They seemed so far away, and so did his old life in Paris. Would Gustave ever see his friends again? French Jews couldn't get the right papers. And without the right papers, how could anyone cross the line, with soldiers like that in charge? Gustave's eyes stung, and he swallowed hard. Suddenly, remembering the leering soldier, he jerked up his coat sleeve and adjusted his watch back to French time. No matter where he was, he promised himself, he would never put his watch on German time again.

18

Saint-Georges, March 1941

Gustave's fingers were too awkward from the cold to turn the pages of his history book. He got up from the kitchen table and stretched. His pants slipped down, and he tugged them back up again. Even though they were getting too short, they were loose around his waist. Food had been in short supply during the winter, and Gustave was getting used to being a little hungry almost all the time. Even on his twelfth birthday, all Maman had been able to make was hard-boiled eggs and rutabaga soup.

Gustave stamped his feet and blew on his fingers to warm them. The winter had been long and bitterly cold, and heating fuel was expensive and scarce. It was especially bad when you had to run outside to the outhouse, but on this March evening, when winter should have been giving way to spring, it seemed to be almost as cold inside the house as it was outside. Even here in the kitchen, the warmest room in the house, Gustave's fingers were numb and stiff.

But it was probably better than living in England, Gustave thought. According to the newspapers, the German bombing there was merciless. Every now and then, Philippe and some of his friends hid behind a wall near the school and lobbed snowballs up into the air so that they plopped down on top of other kids heading toward the building, pretending they were dropping bombs.

"Iiiiaou—pffff!" Philippe had screamed gleefully last week as one fell on Gustave's head, showering bits of snow down the collar of his jacket. "Another bomb hits London!"

Now, remembering the ice on his neck that day, Gustave rubbed his cold fingers under his shirt, massaging his neck and shoulders. Then, without thinking, he shoved his hands into his pockets, the fingers of his left hand feeling for Monkey's warm fur. But his pocket was empty. He usually remembered not to do that anymore because Monkey was never there. Shortly after the soldiers had taken the black radishes, the demarcation line had been closed.

A few weeks ago, the line had opened back up again, but Papa hadn't tried crossing because he had heard that security was very tight. "I'd rather not run into that Boche Georg again," he told them.

So Monkey was still with little Marguerite, and Papa had never gone back to the Roberts' with her boots. Gustave wondered if her tiny feet were cold in the snow. And still no reply had come to Maman's letter to Aunt Geraldine, not even one of those preprinted postcards. What was happening to Jean-Paul and Aunt Geraldine and little Giselle?

What was happening to Marcel and his mother? For years, in Paris, the three families had seen each other almost every day. Now, as month after month went by with no news, Marcel and Jean-Paul and their families seemed to be drifting further and further away.

Gustave's back grew slightly warmer as he leaned on the wall they shared with their landlady. Her kitchen was on the other side, and her stove backed up against the shared wall. After she cooked, the wall stayed warm for a while, radiating heat into the kitchen where Gustave was working. Madame Foncine ate after Gustave's family did, so her kitchen stayed warm later.

It was hard to concentrate, though. Gustave's parents were talking in the living room, and he could overhear most of their conversation, even though they were obviously trying to talk quietly—which, of course, made him try all the harder to hear what they were saying.

"Things are bad in the occupied zone," Papa was saying, almost in a whisper. He added something that Gustave could not hear, and then his voice grew louder. "When I was buying a newspaper today, I heard a man on the street saying to another that Jews in the occupied zone are going to be made to wear badges showing that they are Jews. He was actually glad about it! 'Now we can tell who the Jewish pigs are,' he said. Unbelievable."

"Oh, but that was just one foolish person, Berthold," murmured Maman. "Surely such a thing couldn't happen in France, in a civilized country."

"But people are saying even worse things than that,"

Papa exclaimed. His voice was loud and clear now. "They are putting the foreign Jews into camps. Pétain's government is even doing it here in the unoccupied zone. I heard it again in a café today, and I have heard it enough times that I'm afraid it's true. Whole families—elderly people, small children, women. Imagine trying to survive in unheated barracks in a prison camp in this weather, living in filth and mud. They're saying that people die there every day from the cold, from hunger, and from illness."

Gustave's mother gasped. "Foreign Jews? But the Landaus are from Poland!"

Camps? Gustave thought. Terrible internment camps like the ones he had heard about back in Paris on the newsreel? The French government was doing it too, not just the Nazis? Gustave's pulse raced. How could the citizens of France let them? It was bad enough that the new laws took Jews' jobs away. But to make people live in prison camps, places so horrible that people were dying, just because they were Jewish? He had to do something to stop it, something to fight it. But what? Gustave jumped to his feet, shaking, and paced around the kitchen.

Papa looked in the kitchen doorway. "Finished?" he said to Gustave with strained cheeriness. "Do you want to join us for the BBC broadcast?" He turned to Maman. "It's the best way to find out what's really going on."

Papa adjusted the shortwave knob delicately with his fingertips, finding just the right spot between loud bursts of static. A deep voice sounded in the room. Maman jumped up. "Quieter!" she exclaimed, turning the volume down and eyeing the closed shutters. "Remember, it's illegal to listen to the BBC," she whispered.

"I heard Madame Foncine listening herself the other day. She won't inform on us," Papa answered, but he was speaking quietly too.

"*V* for *victory!*" The hushed words coming from the radio were strong and sure. "On the walls, on the streets, chalk *V* for *victory!*"

Papa smiled grimly. "That should be amusing," he said when the broadcast was over. "The French Resistance wants people to chalk *V*s all over their cities and towns to show how many people want France to overthrow the Nazis. I wonder how many people will dare to do it. It'll be dangerous for anyone the police catch at it. But maybe we'll see a few, even here in Saint-Georges."

Gustave's heart pounded. Yes, he thought fiercely, there were going to be some *V*s in Saint-Georges. He didn't have any chalk. But he was going to do it.

Before he went to bed, Gustave dug out his old box of watercolor paints. He couldn't help glancing at the well that had once held the red paint. Its emptiness was like a taunt. Gustave flipped open his pocketknife and ran the blade around the block of blue paint, then carefully pried it out, keeping it intact, and shoved it deep into the pocket of the pants he would wear to school the next day.

It was dawn when he left for school, leaving a note for his parents. He took a shortcut down a side alley. No one was around. He looked over each shoulder, his fingers grasping the block of paint. With a shaky hand, he marked a large blue *V* on a white wall.

As he turned onto the main road of Saint-Georges, he saw a *V* chalked by someone else on the street and one on the corner of a building. His pulse raced. He ran around to the side of the post office. No one was in sight, and again he marked a large blue *V,* more firmly this time. He looked at it in satisfaction and added the whole word. *"Victoire!"* *Victory!* The letters stood out, bold and blue, on the pale wall. Footsteps sounded on the main road ahead of him, coming closer. Quickly shoving the block of paint into his pocket, Gustave walked back toward the main road. It was the baker, just opening the *boulangerie.* He looked at Gustave for a moment.

"Bonjour, Monsieur," said Gustave, trying to make his voice sound casual and polite, although his heart was pounding.

"Bonjour." The baker nodded. Gustave felt the baker's eyes on his back as he walked on, past the bread bakery and down the road toward the school.

Gustave quickly scrawled three more blue *V*s on the way to school and counted five others done in white chalk by other people. Someone had even put one on the front of the school. Next to the door was a large white *V* and a cross of Lorraine, a vertical line with two crossbars, the symbol of Free France.

Many people here were against the Nazis! Gustave tingled with a fierce joy. He shoved the crumbling remains of the blue paint into his pocket, noticing as he did so that his fingers were slightly stained blue, and ran up the steps into the school.

The school was buzzing with talk. To add to the

confusion, Monsieur Laroche was not in his classroom. The principal put his head in the door, quieting the mounting roar of voices, and directed Gustave's class to join another across the hall. As they carried in chairs and crowded around the few empty desks, Gustave spotted Nicole. She flashed a grin at Gustave. In the front of the classroom, the teacher, a young, slender man with dark hair, looked at the children. His eyes were exultant behind his thick glasses. "I am Monsieur Brunel," he said to Gustave's class. "The homework assignment on the blackboard is for both classes. Please copy it down."

Gustave looked at the blackboard at the front. "Read La Fontaine's 'The League of Rats,'" it said. "Pay special attention to Verses 1–9, Verses 12–15, Verses 27–28." Gustave looked again. Was it his imagination, or did the *V*s on the board look larger and thicker than the other letters? Gustave glanced around the room. A few students scowled down at their work, but many of them were looking at each other and grinning. The teacher caught Gustave's eye and smiled right at him. Gustave smiled back. Then he copied down the homework assignment in his notebook, running his pencil over his own *V*s, making them darker and darker. He stopped only when his pencil point tore a small hole in the paper. His pulse pounded in his fingertips, and he felt as if he could jump up from his desk and run and run.

Nicole looked back at him over her shoulder, her brown eyes sparkling gleefully. Gustave glanced around. All the other kids were working now. No one was watching.

Holding his hand in front of him where only Nicole could see it, he smiled at her and lifted up two blue-stained fingers in a *V* for the flicker of a moment. She flicked her own fingers up in a *V* and smiled back. On her right cheek was a smudge of white chalk.

19

Most of the *V*s done in white chalk washed off in the next rain, but Gustave was glad to see that his *V*s, in the blue watercolor paint, lasted longer. And someone, or maybe several people, put up new chalk *V*s from time to time, often on the school building and the town hall. Gustave's heart always leapt when he saw a new one, especially because the war news was almost always bad now. The Nazis and their allies seemed unstoppable. In April, Gustave would have needed more red paint if he hadn't torn up his map. Yugoslavia and Greece surrendered to the Germans. And at the beginning of June, Maman came home from work with yet more bad news about the new French laws under Pétain.

"The women at work were saying that there's going to be a census of the Jews," she told Papa. "We're going to have to register at the police stations." Sure enough, there was the news in the paper the next day. "The most severe penalties" would be imposed for not following the law. Anyone who didn't register and was caught, French citizen or not, would be interned in a prison camp.

"What are they going to do when they know who is Jewish?" Gustave asked, reading the newspaper over Maman's shoulder as she sat at the kitchen table. It was a warm, sticky evening, but Maman had left the kitchen shutters closed the way she usually did now so that no one could overhear their conversation. Her hands, holding the paper, left damp smudges.

Maman shook her head and sighed. "Nothing good. The new Jewish statute announces more restrictions on Jews. Look." She pointed at another column of type. "Jews are being excluded from more and more professions—law, medicine, pharmacy, architecture. And here it says that only a very limited number of Jewish students will be permitted to attend French universities."

"So even if I do well in school, I might not be able to go to a university?" Gustave exploded. "It isn't fair. I don't think we should register. No one here really knows us. How would they know we're Jewish?"

"Maybe you're right," Papa answered slowly. "As you've said before, Lili, the last name Becker isn't always Jewish."

"I don't know," said Maman. "We don't have a record of being baptized or married by a priest, some people would say we look Jewish, and we don't attend church. What if we don't register and somehow they find out? We could all be put in a camp."

Gustave heard his parents talking late into the night, and by morning they had decided to register.

"I can register our whole family," said Papa. "You don't have to come."

"No," said Maman firmly. "I will come too. But Gustave should wait outside."

Maman put on her best suit and shoes, and she and Papa walked stiffly into the prefecture of police, holding their heads high. Gustave waited in the shade of a tree, watching the shadow get shorter and shorter as noon approached. When his parents came out of the police station, Maman's face was flushed, and not only from the heat.

"Look," she said, holding out the two French identity cards, her hand shaking. "As if we were criminals."

Stamped in large red letters to the right of Maman's photograph, it said *"JUIVE." Jew.* And there it was, above his own name, "BECKER, Gustave," and under his photograph: *"JUIF." Jew.*

Gustave looked at his father.

"They registered me, but they didn't stamp my Swiss identity papers," Papa said quietly. "Apparently, the Swiss government considers that an insult to its citizens."

"So everyone will know we're Jewish now?" Gustave asked on the long walk home to Saint-Georges under the blazing sun. "We don't have to keep it a secret anymore?"

"No, you mustn't tell anyone!" Maman exclaimed. "The fewer people who know, the better."

"Oh, I don't know if we're going to be able to keep it quiet now, Lili," Papa sighed, wiping his sweaty forehead with a handkerchief. "Still, it isn't something to talk about."

The next day at school, Gustave avoided looking at anyone as much as possible, all day. It felt as if the word *"Juif"* were stamped, in red, on his forehead.

At recess, he was sitting alone on the ground, tracing a design in the dirt with a stick, when a shadow fell over him. It was Nicole, and behind her dark silhouette was the white-hot sky.

"Do you want to come over?" she asked. "Claude has a magnifying glass, and we're going to set a piece of paper on fire."

Gustave looked with halfhearted curiosity in the direction she indicated, where Claude and another boy were squatting on the playground.

"No."

"Are you all right?" Nicole asked more hesitantly.

Gustave nodded, glancing past her at the sky, and after a moment, she ran off. A few minutes later, he heard a shriek of triumph from Claude as the paper began to smoke, and then Monsieur Brunel called out scoldingly and ran toward them. Gustave smiled faintly.

He wished he could tell Nicole about the shameful brand on his French identity card. But she wasn't Jewish—nobody else here was—so she wouldn't understand. And even if she would, he wasn't supposed to talk about it.

The long school day came to an end without Gustave's hearing anything about their trip to the prefecture of police, not even from Philippe. And in a week, school was over, without anybody having said anything, so Gustave thought that maybe the prefect at the police station had been discreet. It was possible.

At the end of July, there was another announcement in the paper. Maman read it aloud one humid July evening as they sat at the kitchen table after dinner.

"Now this," she said. "Law number 3086, again with 'the most severe penalties' for noncompliance. 'All Jews must register their place of residence and all their assets with the police.' " She lifted her chin and looked at Papa and Gustave, her eyes glittering. "Now, this I just won't do," she said. "What are they going to do with this information besides take all our money away? That must be what's coming next. How will we survive?"

Papa nodded slowly. "I agree," he said. "They know where we live now. But what if we just register a small amount of money, what we've managed to save from your earnings since we came here, Lili? The money I got when I liquidated the store in Paris—that, we won't register. I'll find a way to buy something valuable with it that's easy to hide."

"We can't live in a country that makes laws like this," Maman murmured. "What is happening with those immigration visas to America?"

Papa got to his feet. "Yes. Enough of this waiting. I'm going to try to get to Lyon to see what I can find out about our visas from the American consulate there."

A week later, Papa started for Lyon, traveling by train. After a few weeks, he came back, tired and disheveled.

"I did what I could," he said wearily after he had bathed in the tin tub Maman had filled for him from the pump in the kitchen, rubbing a towel over his damp hair. "But I don't know what will happen. So many refugees are trying to get into the United States, and they don't want so many Jews." He sighed. "But the affidavit from my cousin has come through. He promises to support our family if we need money. So, we can hope. We may be among the lucky ones."

20

Saint-Georges, September 1941

School began again on a humid day at the end of September. It was hard to believe that he was here again for another school year, Gustave thought, looking around the classroom, remembering that at first Papa had planned for them to be in Saint-Georges for only a few months.

This morning, it was much too hot to learn anything. Gustave looked around and focused on the back of a head with light brown curls. Nicole was in his class this year, and so was Claude. But, unfortunately, Philippe was too. Somehow Gustave just couldn't get away from him.

The teacher was the one Gustave had seen in Nicole's classroom the year before—Monsieur Brunel, the one who had drawn the big, white *V*s on the blackboard. That was good, anyway. This year his class was beginning to learn English, and Monsieur Brunel had just taught them the verb "to be"—"I am," "you are," "he is." It was fun trying to say the strange words. It would be useful if he ever got to America. But it was just too hot to concentrate on English verbs.

Gustave fidgeted and looked at the clock. The other children in the back rows of the schoolroom started to cough and shuffle their feet too as the clock hands inched toward ten-thirty, recess time. Monsieur Brunel looked up from the papers he was correcting and grinned at them.

"OK, kids, put away your books. Recess!" he announced. Gustave jumped up, and the dusty stillness exploded into sudden noise. In the courtyard, Claude came up to Gustave.

"Want to play marbles?" he asked.

"Sure!" said Gustave. "But I don't have any."

"No problem." Claude shrugged. "You can borrow some of mine."

Under the trees on the other side of the courtyard, some other boys were sitting on the ground by a marbles circle. Claude and Gustave sat down with them. Almost immediately, Philippe came up behind them and squeezed into the circle too.

Claude dumped a handful of marbles out of a blue bag and offered them to Gustave. "You can use these."

Claude was a very good player. At the end of his turn, he scooped in a big handful of marbles, laughing. Looking at Claude's heavy bag, Gustave could see why he didn't mind sharing. When it was Gustave's turn, he chose a green glass shooter from the pile Claude had handed him and knocked several marbles out of the ring. One was a beautiful pinkish gray agate. As Gustave reached over to pick them up, Philippe glared at him.

"You think you're going to keep that agate, Jew?" he asked.

One of the marbles slipped out of Gustave's fingers, and he put the others down on the ground before he dropped them too. How did Philippe know? The other boys glanced from Philippe to Gustave.

"Wh-what makes you say I'm a Jew?" Gustave finally stammered.

But he said it just a few beats too late. Philippe snatched his marble. "Jew-thief. My grandfather says the war is all because of the Jews. Jews don't belong in France."

Gustave stood up, but so many thoughts rushed through his head, along with so many reasons not to talk, that he couldn't figure out what to say.

Philippe grinned at Gustave's confusion. "I *knew* it. I knew you were a Jew. But if you're not, then prove it. Unzip!" He jumped up and seized the waist of Gustave's too-loose pants and underwear and yanked them down sharply. Gustave grabbed desperately and pulled them back up, hearing laughter as he did. His face burned. He thought he had caught his pants just in time, but he wasn't sure. Had anyone seen anything? And there were girls around! He *hated* Philippe—*hated* him.

Holding the waistband of his pants in both hands, Gustave walked away stiffly.

Claude started to say something, but Gustave couldn't hear him because of the blood pounding in his ears. How had Philippe guessed that he was Jewish, anyway? If only, when Philippe had first said it, Gustave had stayed calm and suave, like actors in the movies. And now because of the way Gustave had reacted, Philippe knew for sure, even if he hadn't seen anything when he yanked Gustave's pants down. Stupid, stupid! He could have kicked himself for giving it away like that. He walked unsteadily back across the yard and stood with his back against the stones of the school building, wanting to disappear. He blinked sweat out of his eyes, looking unseeingly out at the blur of kids in the yard.

Nicole must have spoken several times before Gustave heard her and turned his head. She was sitting on the steps of the school in a patch of shade. She had lined up some acorns across the stoop and was flicking them down the steps, one by one.

"Philippe's a jerk. Don't let him bother you. Nobody saw anything. His grandfather says that stuff about Jews, and Philippe is always trying to be just like him. Nobody cares what he says."

"Yeah," said Gustave, walking a few steps farther away. Right now, he didn't even feel like talking to Nicole. Maybe especially not Nicole. He stood there a long time, feeling the roughness of the stone wall against his back. His cheeks gradually cooled, but inside him was a hard knot of rage.

After a while, something rustled, and he looked at Nicole. She had a chunk of white bread on her lap, and she was pulling a whole bar of chocolate out of her skirt pocket. Gustave couldn't help staring. Some of the luckier kids, usually ones from farm families, brought food to eat as a snack at recess, but most of the time it was something like a cold baked potato or a hard-boiled egg. Gustave watched as Nicole opened the light green wrapper with "MENIER" written on it in large letters. A whole bar of chocolate! Gustave hadn't seen anyone eating one of those since they'd left Paris. There was never any chocolate for sale in the stores. Menier was his favorite kind of chocolate bar too. He used to buy it in Paris sometimes from kiosks on the street corners when he had pocket money, a long time ago.

Nicole broke off a piece of chocolate, wrapped the rest back up carefully in the silver and green paper, and tucked it back into her pocket. She hollowed out the chunk of bread, pulling out some of the soft inside and eating it. Then she poked the chocolate into the bread and broke off a piece with the chocolate in the middle. She held it out to Gustave.

"Do you want some?" she asked.

"Really?" said Gustave. How could she still want to be friends even after what Philippe had just done to him? Gustave took the bread and chocolate and looked at it in astonishment. "Thanks." He took a bite, tasting the dry mildness of the bread and the vivid, creamy richness of the chocolate on his tongue.

Just then, Philippe ran toward them out of the crowd in the schoolyard, and the sweet taste in Gustave's mouth turned sour.

"Making friends with the Jew-boy?" he sneered at Nicole. He planted himself in front of her, with one hand on his hip, and crooned:

"Viens, poupoule, viens, poupoule, viens!
Le meilleur chocolat, c'est le chocolat POULAIN!"

Come, chickie-chick, come, chickie-chick, and
    try it!
The best chocolate in the world is POULAIN
    chocolate!

Gustave glared at Philippe. Nicole snorted at the familiar jingle for Poulain, a competing brand of chocolate. "I'm not your *poupoule* or anybody else's!" she said. *"GLOU-GLOU-GLOU-GLOU!"* She jumped up and ran a few steps toward Philippe, her short, brown hair bobbing against her cheeks, doing a very creditable imitation of an angry rooster. Philippe swaggered away.

Nicole came back over to Gustave and sat down. "As if he wouldn't jump at the chance to eat Menier chocolate or any other kind if he had it," she remarked to Gustave.

Gustave managed a slight grin. "Where did you get the chocolate, anyway?" he asked after a moment, licking his fingers.

"My father works for the Menier family at Chenonceau, and sometimes the Meniers used to give the people who work there a few chocolate bars. We still have one or two left. Do you know Chenonceau? That castle belongs to the Meniers. Bought with chocolate money."

"A castle?"

"Yes, haven't you seen it? It's right nearby. It is the most beautiful castle in France."

Gustave grinned at Nicole's sudden transformation from tough village girl to cultured tour guide. Nicole laughed.

"Well, that's what I've heard people say, anyway. I haven't seen *every* castle in France. But Chenonceau is only a few kilometers from here. Do you want to go there with me some Sunday afternoon? Can you get a bicycle? We could bike over and see the outside from down the river."

Just then, the teacher came out on the steps and rang the bell, calling everyone in. As the students lined up, Gustave thought about going to see Chenonceau. Maybe his parents would let him use the bicycle if he promised to be careful with it. He could hardly believe that Nicole had shared her chocolate with him. He grinned to himself. Marcel, who liked to roar and grunt and squeak while making shadow animals on the wall with his fingers, would really appreciate a girl who could imitate a rooster like that. But as Gustave turned to walk through the classroom door, something banged into his shoulder, hard. Philippe pushed through the door ahead of him.

"Veuillez m'excuser, Monsieur!" Philippe said, with mock politeness—*Be so good as to excuse me, sir!* The teacher glanced in their direction. Gustave flushed with rage and thought about the other, less pleasant thing he would have to tell Maman and Papa this evening. If someone in the village suspected that they were Jews, that probably meant that everyone else did too. And even if, by some miracle, no one else already knew that they were Jewish because they had registered with the police, now Philippe would make sure that everyone did.

But Gustave forgot all about school as soon as he got home. Papa, who had spent the afternoon at a café, arrived at the front gate at the same time that Gustave did, and Maman came bursting out of the house.

"Look! From Geraldine!" she cried, waving the yellow postcard in the air.

Maman couldn't stop fingering the card and talking about it, even during dinner. "Finally, after a whole year, we get word from her!" she said, ladling out the soup. "But it doesn't sound good. Not good at all."

Gustave took a bite of bread and examined the yellow postcard, the kind the Germans made people use for mail across the demarcation line. "Strictly for family correspondence" was printed at the top. "Write nothing outside the lines." You could choose from a few preprinted messages, circling the ones that applied and crossing out the ones that did not. Aunt Geraldine had crossed out "ill" and "wounded." "Geraldine, Jean-Paul, and Giselle" filled the blank line on the postcard before the words "are in good health." Aunt Geraldine had written in "David" before "is a prisoner of war." That was to be expected, because no one had heard of any of the captured French soldiers coming home yet.

"Look!" said Gustave. "She circled both 'Kisses' and 'Affectionate thoughts,' but you're only supposed to circle one of them. It's lucky that the Boches didn't throw the card away because of that. But maybe she did the same thing before and that kept her postcards from getting through to us."

"Oh, how ridiculous! But you might be right," Maman said, peering over Gustave's shoulder. "But what could she mean by this?"

There were only two blank lines at the bottom where people could write in their own words. In a shaky hand, Aunt Geraldine had written: "The neighbors are away. We think they are on vacation. Your advice was correct. We may have to go on vacation next." Below, she had signed her name, still in shaky handwriting: "Geraldine."

" 'The neighbors' must mean the Landaus," Gustave said. "And 'your advice was correct' must mean that she realizes they should have come to Saint-Georges. Even though it's the country and there are outhouses."

Maman smiled faintly. "That makes sense," she agreed. "But 'on vacation'? No one is going 'on vacation' now." She picked up the card and ran her finger over the curving loops of Aunt Geraldine's signature. "And the Landaus never had enough money for that sort of thing in the best of times." Her bowl of soup cooled on the table in front of her, untouched.

"No," said Papa. He put down his spoon.

"It's as if she is making up a code," said Maman. "What is she hinting at? And what does she mean that she and the children 'may have to go on vacation next'?"

"I'm not sure," said Papa slowly, wiping his lips with his napkin. "Maybe it means the Landaus have gone into hiding to get away from the Germans. But I'm afraid—" He glanced at Gustave and hesitated. Then he went on. "I'm afraid it may mean that the Germans have arrested them for being Jews."

Maman gave a faint cry.

Gustave's stomach lurched, threatening to send his soup back up. Marcel and his mother, arrested? In one of those prison camps? Somewhere filthy and crowded, without enough food or clothes, without heat in winter, without doctors if they got sick? A place run by brutal Nazi soldiers with rifles, who hated Jews? Gustave wanted to scream. He felt as if he were falling into a deep, dark hole.

"We must get your sister and the children out of Paris." Papa's voice sounded from far away, pulling Gustave back. "Soon. Immediately. But how can we get them across the demarcation line without papers?" he added, drumming his fingers on the table. "I just don't know any reliable way."

"What about Marcel?" Gustave cried. "We don't know

for sure that Aunt Geraldine means that they were arrested by the Germans. Maybe the Landaus are away visiting relatives, and that's what she means by 'on vacation.' We have to help them too!"

Maman sighed. "I'll write Geraldine one of those yellow postcards, saying that we are all well but earnestly wish for a reunion of the family and our dear friends. She will know what that means, and if she can contact the Landaus, she can tell Marcel's family again that we want them to come. I'll also write a postcard to Marcel's mother. But even if they get the postcards, without passes from the Germans, how can either family get out of the occupied zone?"

Gustave thought about that question for what seemed like most of the night. Marcel and his mother had to still be in Paris. They had to. Maman and Papa must be wrong about them being arrested by the Nazis. What Aunt Geraldine wrote had to mean something else. But even if they could leave Paris and travel until they were at the other side of the river Cher, how could they cross the demarcation line?

Maybe there was a lonely stretch of the river where the Germans didn't patrol, and Marcel and Jean-Paul and their mothers could swim across some dark night. But what about the baby? She could drown. Could they find a boat instead? But boats were forbidden, "on pain of death." The Germans had destroyed or confiscated all the boats they could find. Could Jean-Paul's family and the Landaus somehow sneak over a bridge? But how, when they were so heavily guarded at all hours of the day and night? Gustave twisted and turned in bed, running over and over possible plans in his mind, but he couldn't think of any safe way to smuggle two mothers, two boys, and a baby girl across the line.

Gustave had almost forgotten about Philippe, but he remembered what he had done during the marbles game as soon as he walked into the classroom the next day. Philippe smirked at Gustave from across the room, gesturing as if he were yanking Gustave's pants down again, then turned to whisper something to the boy next to him. The boy glanced up at Gustave and laughed. Gustave glowered and looked down, digging his pencil hard into the wood of his desk. Don't be conspicuous, Papa had said when Gustave had started school there over a year ago. Don't get into arguments. Had Papa known how hard it would be to do that?

Gustave avoided Philippe at recess, and at the end of the day, he hurried away from the school. When he heard feet running behind him, he tensed. Was it Philippe, planning to beat him up? He turned, clenching his hands into fists. But it was Nicole.

"Do you want to walk together?" she asked when she had caught up with Gustave.

Gustave unclenched his hands. "Oh. Sure."

"Can you believe how much math we have to do tonight?" she asked. "*And* a test to study for! Already!" Gustave shrugged. He could hardly pay attention to Nicole when he kept expecting Philippe to jump out at him. But nothing happened.

At her turnoff, Nicole paused. "Listen," she said, looking around to make certain that no one was nearby. Her voice was suddenly hushed and serious. "What Philippe said yesterday in the schoolyard—it was true, wasn't it? Your family is Jewish?"

Gustave flinched. But everybody was going to know now, anyway. And the way she said it was very different from the way Philippe had. "Yes," he answered, making himself look her straight in the eye. "We are."

Nicole nodded. "But aren't you going to try to leave France?" she went on in a whisper. "My father says it's getting really dangerous for Jews here."

Nicole's face was so honest and worried. And she had had that smudge of white chalk on her cheek that day last spring. And on La Toussaint last fall, she had so conveniently and persistently changed the subject away from bacon and Catholic festivities. Suddenly, Gustave was very sure that he could trust her. "Well, it's not that easy," he said. "Besides, my aunt and cousins—they're on the other side of the demarcation line. So are my best friend and his mother."

"I thought it might be something like that." Nicole tossed her hair out of her face, smiling. "So, can you get a bike? Are you going to come on Sunday?"

"I think so," said Gustave, a little bewildered by Nicole's rapid mood changes. "I'll check tonight."

"OK, see you." She ran up the hill, her schoolbag swinging on her shoulder.

Gustave wasn't sure if he should ask about borrowing Maman's bike, with everyone so worried about Jean-Paul's family and Marcel's. But at dinner, Papa asked him how school was going this year, and he spilled out everything—about what Philippe had said, and about Nicole and the chocolate and going to see Chenonceau.

"I'm glad you have a new friend," said Maman, distractedly. "Yes, you can take the bicycle. But don't let it out of your sight for a moment. A woman who works with me had hers stolen last week, and now she has to walk to work."

"Don't you think this boy Philippe might just have been curious about you?" asked Papa. "The villagers have all lived here for many generations, and then we move in just before the Germans invade Paris. Of course they wonder why we're living here. They may even wonder if we're Jewish. It isn't surprising that some people are curious."

"Philippe isn't just curious. He said that Jews are to blame for the war. Nicole said his grandfather believes it too."

"I don't like hearing that," said Papa, slowly. "I don't like hearing that at all."

That night, the rain began and continued for two days. When the sky cleared, the sticky summer was over, wet, yellow leaves were strewn on the ground, and it felt as if it had always been fall. In the evening of the day that the rain stopped, when the landlady was away and no one seemed to be around in the house next door, Gustave's parents showed him a small metal box. Inside it, in small cloth bags, were a roll of American dollar bills, Maman's few pieces of jewelry, and two shapeless stones.

"This is the rest of our valuable property that we didn't declare to the police," said Papa. "Although they don't look like it, those stones are precious jewels. They haven't been cut and polished yet. I exchanged most of our money from the liquidation of the shoe store for these uncut stones. Tonight, we are going to hide everything."

Gustave nodded, his mouth dry. The three of them went out together into the yard behind the house, Maman carrying the box in both hands. On the far side of an old chicken coop that was no longer in use, Papa dug a hole in the rain-softened earth. Maman handed him the box. Papa buried it deep in the ground, stamping on the earth. Gustave helped him strew gravel and leaves over the surface so that no one could see that it had been disturbed. Then Papa walked Gustave back to the house and had him find the spot where the box was buried.

After Gustave found the spot a second time without any trouble, even though by then it was almost completely dark, Papa put both of his hands on Gustave's shoulders and looked straight into his eyes. "Don't tell anyone where it is," Papa said. "But remember."

"But you and Maman know where it is too," said Gustave, glancing at his mother. She turned her head away, looking silently into the darkness.

"Yes. But the day might come when you need to remember it all by yourself," Papa said. His voice was low and hoarse. "You might need money. These days, things could happen. You need to be strong and brave and know how to take care of yourself. Maman and I need to know that you will remember where it is."

Gustave stared at Papa. Take care of himself? Did Papa think that their family could be arrested and put in a camp, even though they had registered at the prefecture of police? Or that just his parents would be taken, leaving Gustave on his own? Gustave looked at his parents, standing there in the dusk. He felt suddenly hollowed out inside and so cold that it seemed as if he would never be warm again.

He reached out and put his hand on his father's coat sleeve, the way he used to when he was younger, feeling its familiar rough texture. Gustave and his parents gazed together into the darkness.

"I will remember where it is," he said.

That Sunday, a beautiful, crisp October day with a gust-ing wind, Gustave pedaled his mother's bicycle to the outskirts of the village where Nicole lived.

A tall man pushing a wheelbarrow came around the side of the barn and waved to Gustave as he came up the hill. Nicole came out of the shed, wheeling a bicycle. It was rusty, definitely older than Gustave's, and it had a wicker basket on the handlebars.

"Papa said I had to take this one today," she grumbled cheerfully. "He needs to use the good one. Look at this front tire. It is a makeshift occupation model. I'm going to go about as fast as a snail."

Gustave looked more closely at the front tire, which was oddly bulky.

"What's wrong with it?" he asked.

"Oh, we got so many flats that we couldn't patch it up any more. And since you can't buy a new tire because of the war, my father put another flat tire over the first one. It's just two flat tires, one over the other, with no air inside. It's really bumpy to ride."

Nicole's father walked over and patted her affectionately on the back. "Oh, stop complaining!" he said. He had a long, narrow face with a warm smile and crinkly eyes.

"*Bonjour*, Monsieur Morin," said Gustave, reaching out his hand.

Monsieur Morin shook it. "It's very nice to meet you, Gustave," he said. "Have fun, kids. And Nicole, be sensible. You have your hat?"

Why was he asking that? Gustave wondered. It was very obvious that Nicole had a blue beret on her short, brown curls. But Nicole nodded, and she and Gustave waved goodbye and biked off down the hill. As soon as they were out of sight of her father, Nicole pedaled faster, then lifted her hands up into the air, flinging her legs out to the side and shrieking with glee. Her bike rattled down the bumpy hill, faster and faster, the fenders clanking.

Gustave grinned. Once, Marcel had borrowed a pair of roller skates from a kid at school and rolled down the steepest hill he could find. He had crashed at the bottom, scraping both his knees raw, but he had said it was worth it for the thrill of the ride. He hadn't done it again, though.

"Good thing your father didn't see you do that! What if you hit a rock?" Gustave said, laughing, when he caught up with her at the bottom.

"Oh, I just like a little excitement," answered Nicole.

The route Nicole took to Chenonceau seemed very roundabout. When they went through the villages, she slowed down and wound up one street and then down the next, craning her neck from side to side as if she were looking for someone or something. Outside a café, she stopped to pat a small black-and-white mutt that came out into the street, wagging its tail to greet her.

"*Bonjour,* Victoire!" she said to the dog. Gustave let Victoire sniff his feet and around his bike, then leaned down to pat her.

A small, wiry elderly man came out of the café.

"Who's your friend, Nicole?" he asked, peering at the two of them.

"This is Gustave. He's in my class at school," Nicole answered. "Gustave, this is Monsieur Ferrand. Victoire is his dog."

Monsieur Ferrand shook Gustave's hand, looked him over, and nodded.

"How is business today, quiet or busy?" Nicole asked.

"Oh, very quiet, as far as I have seen," said Monsieur Ferrand. Gustave looked at the café. He could see what Monsieur Ferrand meant. Only one man sat at a table, drinking a cup of coffee—probably the fake barley coffee that was all anyone had now—and reading a book.

"Well, thanks, see you later," said Nicole. She led the way around the corner and down several streets, then away from the village. After riding for several kilometers, she stopped, facing what looked to Gustave like nothing more than a long stretch of woods.

"That's the edge of the Chenonceau grounds," she said, getting off her bike.

"Oh," said Gustave, disappointed. "I thought we were going to be able to see the castle."

"We can, from down the river," Nicole answered. "We'll go there next. I just want to rest here for a moment." She reached into her bicycle basket, pulled out a white hand-knit wool cap, took off her blue beret, and put on the cap. Gustave got off his bike and laid it down by the side of the road. He was puzzled. Nicole didn't seem tired enough to want to rest.

"Why do you have that other hat?" he asked.

"Oh, you know parents," said Nicole, looking away and pulling the hat down more firmly around her ears. "My father always thinks I'll catch cold, and this white one is warmer."

"Oh," said Gustave. The day was windy, but he didn't think it was *that* cold. And why hadn't Nicole's father told her to wear that one when they started off, before they had gotten warmed up from biking? Nicole seemed to be watching for something in the Chenonceau woods. After a minute, she turned and noticed Gustave's bewildered expression. Nicole dropped her bike and sat on a rock near him.

"That dog Victoire used to be a stray," Nicole said. "You want to hear how Monsieur Ferrand adopted her and how she got that name?"

"Sure," said Gustave, glad that Nicole was acting more normal.

"You know how the Nazis made it illegal for people in the occupied zone to fly the French flag or even wear the French colors? Well, last summer, Victoire didn't have a name. She was just a stray dog who was always nosing around. So some boys around here caught her and painted her tail blue, white, and red, the colors of the French flag, and sent her over the bridge. Monsieur Ferrand saw it happen. Victoire went right under the barrier over the road, into the occupied zone, right by the Germans' sentry box. The German soldier was so mad. He took out his rifle to shoot the dog."

Gustave remembered Jacques, the pony, dead on the national highway, his mane in a pool of blood, shot by the Germans in the airplane. "On *purpose* he was going to shoot a dog? That's so stupid! How was it the dog's fault?" His voice came out sounding so angry that Nicole looked surprised.

"Yes, on purpose. It made Monsieur Ferrand furious too. So he stood at this end of the bridge and whistled for the dog to come back. And then he yelled, *'Victoire! Victoire! Victoire!'* Victory! Victory! Victory! The German soldier stopped pointing his gun at the dog and pointed it at Monsieur Ferrand. 'Is there a problem, officer?' says Monsieur Ferrand innocently. 'Am I not permitted to call my dog?' The soldier couldn't do anything about that. So now the dog belongs to Monsieur Ferrand, and her name is Victoire. Monsieur Ferrand calls her anytime he sees a German soldier. Or when he sees Philippe's grandfather, that Nazi sympathizer. Philippe's grandfather shakes and turns purple, he gets so mad!" Nicole was laughing so hard, she almost fell off the rock.

"So the soldier put away his rifle?" Gustave wanted to hear about the dog, not about that moron Philippe and his grandfather.

"His rifle? Oh—no. He shot at Victoire as she was running back over the bridge."

"Who would do that? What's the point of shooting a dog? I mean, what is the *point*?" Gustave's voice shook.

"No point. But a Nazi would do it. You don't need to get so upset, though." Nicole looked at him, confused, twisting a lock of hair around her finger. "Victoire is clever and fast. She got away."

Gustave thought about the friendly, curious little dog and shuddered. What if she hadn't been quite so quick or so lucky? "Come on—let's go see the castle," he said. He didn't want to think any more about the Nazis and their guns.

Nicole got back on her bike. As they pedaled off, Gustave heard a stick crack and turned his head. Four people—a man, two women, and a teenaged boy—were coming out of the woods. The four of them hurried across the road, then started to walk along it as if they were just out for a stroll. But they looked strangely bulky, as if they were wearing several layers of clothes under their coats, and two of them carried small suitcases.

"Nicole?" said Gustave, gesturing with his head.

Nicole turned and looked back for a moment. "Oh. Yeah," she said, not sounding surprised. But she didn't stop riding until they had arrived at a spot where you could see the river.

"Down there," she said, pointing.

Gustave looked. A graceful castle stretched all the way across the river Cher. Its delicate white arches cast their reflection into the serene water flowing underneath. It almost seemed to be floating on top of the river. It was like something from a fairy tale, a castle built on top of the water.

"*Formidable!*" said Gustave. "That's amazing! It must be like living in a boat."

"Yes." Nicole looked around them and lowered her voice, even though they were alone. "But you know what's really amazing? Monsieur Menier wakes up in the occupied zone, on the other side of the river, then gets up, stretches, takes a little stroll through his house—and he's on this side of the river, in the free zone."

Gustave looked back at Nicole, puzzled. What was she trying to tell him?

"Imagine how convenient that is for Monsieur Menier," Nicole added. "Or how convenient it is for his *visitors*." She emphasized the last word, still looking hard at Gustave. "Maybe you know someone who might like to pay him a visit. His guests walk into his house from Occupied France. Then they walk out of his grounds here, and they are in the unoccupied zone."

Gustave stared at Nicole. Suddenly everything was starting to make sense. The "visitors" came out of the woods on the edge of Monsieur Menier's grounds, maybe carrying suitcases because they were in the middle of a long journey, and found that they were safely across the river, in the unoccupied zone. Yes, he knew some people who would like to visit Monsieur Menier—Jean-Paul's family and the Landaus! But Gustave and his parents didn't know rich people like the Meniers.

Nicole smiled at him. "Isn't it great that someone has a house like that? Someone my father works for?"

Of course. Gustave and his parents didn't know the Meniers. But Nicole and her father did.

"My father says that your father should come and talk to him," Nicole said. "Tomorrow."

23

When Gustave got home from school the next day, Papa was dancing Maman around the small kitchen, singing.

"Stop, stop!" Maman finally cried, pulling away and laughing. "I'm getting dizzy!"

Papa thumped Gustave on the back. "Well done, well done!" he said, bouncing on his toes.

"Shhh!" said Maman. But her face, like Papa's, was flushed, and she smiled in a way that Gustave hadn't seen in a long time.

Papa dropped his voice to a whisper. "Nicole's father, Monsieur Morin, he's such a good man! He's part of the French Resistance. He has contacts, and he's going to see about getting Aunt Geraldine and the kids across the line to meet us here. He'll try to find out where the Landaus are and convey the message to them too."

"They'll go through Chenonceau, won't they?" asked Gustave.

"That's it! Nicole's father has connections with some people on the other side of the line. They'll make contact with Geraldine and Madame Landau and help them come with the children to the Roberts' farm. Monsieur Morin knows the Robert family, and they sometimes help people escape. Madame Robert and her mother will put them all up for the night, and then one of Monsieur Morin's contacts will smuggle them in, right through the castle and over the river!"

"And today, to top it all off," Maman beamed, "we heard that the affidavit from Papa's cousin did the trick! We have immigration visas to the United States, for our family and also Geraldine's! We're going to America!"

"If we succeed in getting the Landaus to Saint-Georges, they will have to stay in France," said Papa. "But they'll be safer here in the unoccupied zone, and Monsieur Morin said he'll do what he can to help them if things get worse for the Jews."

Gustave couldn't sit still to study. He and Papa went outside and kicked around an old, partially flat soccer ball that Gustave had found in the corner of the garage.

Papa whooped every time he made a goal. They stayed out until the sun sank, smoldering pink and orange, beneath the horizon. Gustave breathed in deep gulps of the cold air as they headed in, panting and laughing. Before too long, Jean-Paul and Marcel would be there, playing soccer with them, Gustave thought. Giselle must be a lot bigger now. Aunt Geraldine would be kissing him soon, and he wouldn't even mind. And she and Maman and Madame Landau would sit chatting in the living room for hours and hours. Soon the three families would all be together again, just like before, at least for a little while.

As he and Papa walked under the second hazelnut tree, Gustave jumped up and touched a branch high above him. A star twinkled, bright and far away, in the cold night sky overhead.

Gustave knew that he couldn't discuss the escape plan outside the house, not even with Nicole. Someone might overhear. But when his eyes met Nicole's across the room in school the next morning, he couldn't help smiling. When he saw her, he thought immediately of Chenonceau. Soon Jean-Paul and Marcel and their mothers and little Giselle would be creeping through the luxurious rooms of the castle, with the river Cher flowing, cold and deep, beneath them. Maybe they would see big rooms with enormous fireplaces and tapestries with unicorns and forest scenes. Maybe Monsieur Menier would invite the ladies to sit on a delicate gilded sofa with velvet cushions. Aunt Geraldine could rest, warming herself by the fire, holding Giselle asleep on her lap, with Madame Landau seated comfortably beside her. Maybe a cook would come out of the kitchen with a basket full of green-wrapped Menier chocolate bars for Jean-Paul and Marcel to stuff into their coat pockets.

Gustave was so busy thinking about Chenonceau that

he didn't immediately notice the note on his desk. When he did see it, he unfolded it eagerly, thinking it might be from Nicole. But what he saw, on a piece of paper torn out of a notebook, was an enormous, dark swastika. Beneath it, in big, black letters, were the words *"Hitler a raison! Exterminons les juifs!"* Hitler is right! Death to the Jews!

Gustave's fingers went cold down to the bone. He looked up, and the room seemed to swirl around him.

A hand closed over his shoulder. "What is this?" said Monsieur Brunel, looking down at Gustave's desk. Gustave heard his sudden intake of breath. Monsieur Brunel picked up the note between his thumb and forefinger, holding it out to the class at arm's length as if it were something filthy.

"Who wrote this?" he asked. His voice was quiet but full of controlled fury. "Who put this disgraceful note on Gustave's desk?"

No one spoke. Gustave's pulse beat so furiously that he could feel it shaking his whole body. Slowly, he turned his head and scowled at Philippe. Monsieur Brunel, following Gustave's gaze, looked at Philippe too. Philippe's mouth twitched, but the rest of his face was stony and hard, his eyes burning back at Gustave.

"No one will admit to doing this?" Monsieur Brunel paused, staring at Philippe, but none of the students said anything. "Then whoever wrote this is also a coward."

The class remained silent. Monsieur Brunel crumpled the note in his fist. "Tonight," he thundered, "you will all write an essay on the meaning of the motto of the French Republic: *Liberté, Égalité, Fraternité.*" Monsieur Brunel pounded his hand down on Gustave's desk as he spoke the last three words, pausing after each one. "Liberty. Equality. Fraternity. These are the values of our republic. I expect each one of you to think long and hard about what they mean."

Philippe raised his hand.

"Yes, Philippe?" said Monsieur Brunel coldly.

"Excuse me, sir." Philippe's voice was obsequiously polite. "Don't you mean you want us to write on the *new* slogan of Vichy France: Work, Family, Fatherland? The slogan that shows our Aryan values and our cooperation with the Germans?" He pointed up at the spot where the picture of Maréchal Pétain, with his white mustache, hung on the classroom wall. "The Maréchal is the leader of France now. I'm sure he would want us to write on the new slogan."

Monsieur Brunel's eyes burned down at Philippe. "*I* am the teacher here," he said. "You will write on the subject *I* assign. And *you*, Philippe," he added, his voice steely, "in your essay, *you* will devote particular attention to explaining the meaning of equality. Equality among all people. And write carefully about our French value of fraternity too," he said, looking around the room. "Brotherhood. Unless we treat each other as equals and as brothers or sisters, we cannot have true liberty."

Across the room, Nicole's eyes flashed triumphantly at Gustave. Gustave's whole body had gone numb now, and he couldn't make himself smile back. Philippe was looking across the room too, glaring. He would be even angrier now. If, for no reason, Philippe could write a note like that, who knew what else he could do.

A few days later, Gustave walked home from school, his rucksack over his shoulder, kicking a stone ahead of him with his foot. His mother had asked him to buy any bread the baker had at the *boulangerie,* even one of the dark, gritty loaves made from poor-quality flour that were usually all they had now. But that day the baker's shelves had been completely empty. That meant no bread of any kind for dinner. As Gustave turned the corner, he could see that at the top of the hill, in front of his house, there was some sort of commotion in the street. Partway up the hill, in the road, three small children he didn't know were chattering excitedly.

"What's going on?" Gustave asked. One of the two boys had a green yo-yo, and the little girl was sucking on her finger.

"They're raiding that house," said the taller boy, proud to have the information. "It's those Jews from Paris. They've been using curtains to signal to British planes from the attic. Someone informed the police." The boy turned and pointed up the road. The little girl took her finger out of her mouth.

Gustave shoved past them and tore up the hill. Signaling from the attic? A raid?

"Marc! That boy lives there!" he heard the little girl exclaim behind him.

Madame Foncine was just outside the front gate, her hands on her hips, scowling. Gustave's parents stood together in the middle of the road. Maman's face was blotchy from weeping. The police chief stood next to Papa, gripping his arm. Papa was pale, and his broad shoulders were stooped like an old man's. Gustave suddenly noticed how thin Papa had grown. Another policeman opened the front door from the inside, shouted something up the stairs, and threw a chest out into the yard, where it landed with a thud, cracking open and spilling blankets out onto the ground.

Gustave dashed toward the gate, his breath coming in gasps. The policeman holding Papa turned to look at Gustave. "Halt!" he barked. "Where are *you* going?"

"There's no way up!" Gustave shouted at him. "Just look and see! There's no way up to the attic from our side of the house! How could we signal to anybody?"

The policeman turned to Madame Foncine. "Is that true, what the boy says?" he barked again.

Madame Foncine stood with her feet apart, an apron over her dress, her face scarlet with fury. "The attic?" she yelled at him. "That's what this is all about? What's wrong with the attic? What he says is true. The only way up is from *my* side of the house! Stop this foolishness right now!" she stormed.

The police chief dropped Papa's arm and walked over to Madame Foncine. "I apologize for the disruption, Madame," he said. "But how were we to know that? We had to investigate the report."

"Your men are hoodlums!" Madame Foncine wasn't in any mood to listen. "Servants to the Boches! You come in here and smash up my furniture! It belongs to me, a French-woman! The Jews are renters!"

"Excuse us, Madame," said the police chief. "Evidently it was a false report."

The chief called into the house, and his men came out. They walked away, saying nothing to either of Gustave's parents.

When they were all gone, Madame Foncine stomped back in, still muttering, and Maman and Papa walked slowly back into the house. Gustave followed. When he saw the state of the living room, he gasped. It was a shambles. Drawers had been emptied, cushions slashed, objects tossed around the room. The glass front of the armoire was shattered. Smashed china and broken glass were strewn all over the floor. He found his Boy Scout manual open and facedown, under a broken clock. The page with the pictures of knots was crumpled and torn.

Up in his room, the bed was overturned, and the drawers of the dresser were pulled out and flipped over, their contents on the floor. The framed photograph of Gustave and Marcel and Jean-Paul that had stood on the dresser was gone. Gustave finally found it under the bed. The glass was cracked. Gustave picked it up, holding the cool metal of the frame. He carefully picked out the shards of glass and put them into the wastebasket. The photo inside was ripped, right across Marcel's face. It looked as if someone had ground a boot heel into it. Gustave could still see the snowy mountains in the background and his own face and Jean-Paul's, but Marcel's face was gone. Tears stung Gustave's eyes. He cradled the damaged photograph in his hands and slowly walked back downstairs.

Maman had the broom out and was sweeping up the debris. Papa righted an overturned armchair and sat down on it heavily. "It's a good thing we buried the valuables when we did," he said. "The police would have confiscated them if they had found them."

"Who would denounce us?" Maman asked, her voice wobbly.

"Who knows?" said Papa. His words were so quiet that Gustave could hardly hear them. "It doesn't even matter. But we have to leave."

"With Geraldine and her children," said Maman.

"Yes," said Papa. "All of us. We will wait until they arrive. But no longer."

"Papa?" said Gustave shakily from the doorway. "What about the Landaus? Won't they be coming with Jean-Paul's family?"

Papa sighed. "I'm sure they'll come if Monsieur Morin's contacts can find them," he said. "And if they can't, we'll see what Geraldine knows when they get here. If she doesn't know where they are, I'm afraid there is nothing we can do to help them. But one thing is absolutely clear. We have to get out of France. Immediately."

25

Philippe stood with his arms folded across his chest, blocking the doorway to the classroom.

"How are you today, Gustave?" he asked in the fake polite voice Gustave had heard him use before. "And your family—how is your family? Your mother and father—they are well?"

Gustave stared at him in silence. Philippe. Of course. It had been Philippe—probably with his grandfather—who had informed on them to the police. Gustave pushed by Philippe and ran into the classroom, looking for Nicole. But she wasn't there. She didn't arrive, not even after the late bell rang. It was a long, dreary day of school without her.

"Will you stay for a minute after class?" Monsieur Brunel asked Gustave when the bell rang to signal the end of school.

Gustave put his books into his schoolbag and went up to Monsieur Brunel's desk as the other kids hurried out the door. When the room had emptied, Monsieur Brunel stood up and put his hand on Gustave's shoulder. His face was troubled.

"I heard about what happened at your house yesterday, and I wanted you to know how very sorry I am," he said. "How are your parents?"

"They're fine, I guess," said Gustave, looking down at the floor.

"That's good." Monsieur Brunel turned to the pile of papers on his desk. "I have something I need you to do for me. Nicole's father sent me a note saying that she stayed home from school today because she isn't feeling well. He asked if you would bring her today's homework." He grinned suddenly at Gustave. "We both know that Nicole would never want to fall behind in her studies."

Gustave mustered up the energy to smile back at him, faintly. Homework. Oh, yeah, Nicole *sure* wouldn't want to miss any of *that*.

"Oui, Monsieur," he said, picking up the papers. "I'll bring it to her." At least he would get to see Nicole today after all.

As Gustave trudged up the hill to the Morins' house, he wondered if she had heard about the raid. It was Nicole who opened the door. She was pale but smiling, and her left arm was in a sling.

"What happened?" asked Gustave.

"I broke my collarbone. Come on in," Nicole replied.

"Does it hurt?" asked Gustave, following her into the

kitchen. He was surprised to see Monsieur Morin leaning back in a chair at the kitchen table. Two hats, Nicole's blue beret and the white hand-knit cap, were on the table in front of him.

Monsieur Morin stood up and pulled out a chair. "Hello, Gustave," he said. "Sit down. We need to talk."

"As you can see," Monsieur Morin began, "Nicole had an accident, and—"

"I made a ramp with some old boards," Nicole interrupted. "You should have seen me fly when I bicycled off it—until I crashed!"

Monsieur Morin sighed affectionately, patting Nicole's head. "The doctor says she must keep the arm still. So that means no running around, no tree climbing, no jumping off chicken coops with a blanket for a parachute"—he grinned at Nicole—"and no bike riding." He looked steadily at Gustave. "As you might have suspected, Nicole sometimes does some important riding on her bicycle."

Gustave's breath caught in his throat. "That white hat Nicole put on when we were in sight of the Chenonceau grounds—it meant something, didn't it?" he asked.

"Yes," said Monsieur Morin, his voice low and steady. "Nicole works with me for the French Resistance, helping people escape from the Nazis. I receive word from my connection over the river that 'visitors' are coming to Chenonceau. When the visitors are passing through the château, Nicole rides through the villages nearby to be sure there are no German soldiers or police around, or anyone who looks suspicious. No one pays any attention to a girl riding her bike. If the coast is clear, she puts on the

176

white hat, signaling to the visitors that it is safe to go on. Then they follow the directions they have been given and meet their next connection at the designated meeting point. This person helps them continue their journey. We don't know anything about the person who helps them next. It is safer for everyone that way."

"I knew it!" Gustave exclaimed. "I knew some of it, I mean. I knew there was something funny going on with that hat."

"We just got word that Nicole should ride through the town late this afternoon," Monsieur Morin went on. "There are some visitors at Chenonceau who will be moving on this evening. We could send an adult. But a child on a bicycle is much less likely to be noticed." Monsieur Morin paused for a moment and looked intently at Gustave. "It *is* a dangerous responsibility," he added. "I'm sure you understand that. You don't have to do it. But Nicole thought you might be willing to ride instead of her. I tried to check with your parents, but no one was home when I went by."

Gustave took a deep breath. At last, at last, something he could do. "I can decide for myself. I'll do it," he said firmly, his heart pounding.

"You remember the way we went, right?" Nicole leaned forward. "You have to stop and speak to Monsieur Ferrand and ask, 'How is business today, quiet or busy?' If he says that business has been quiet, he hasn't seen any police or any Germans. You go on, and then you stop across from the woods. If everything is clear, you change to the white hat."

"But if you see *anything* suspicious," Monsieur Morin continued, "if you see a German soldier, or even a French policeman, or if Monsieur Ferrand says, 'The café has been bustling,' or if anything unusual seems to be going on, you keep the blue beret on your head."

"I've always put on the white hat," admitted Nicole. "It has always been quiet."

"Still, better safe than sorry," said Monsieur Morin. "If you aren't sure, keep the blue beret on."

Nicole picked up the beret and placed it on Gustave's head with her one good hand. It slid down over his nose. She laughed and adjusted it. Gustave's face tingled where her hand brushed his cheek.

"There!" Nicole laughed. "No one will notice a French boy riding an old bicycle and wearing a blue beret."

Gustave nodded and glanced at her for a moment, his cheeks burning, then dropped his eyes. His breath came quickly.

Monsieur Morin went out to the shed with Gustave to get the bicycle. He tucked the white hat in a canvas bag and put it into the wicker bicycle basket.

"Thank you, Gustave," he said. "What you are doing is very important. You need to be at the spot opposite the woods by four forty-five. Do you have a watch?"

Gustave held up his wrist.

"Good. It's getting late, so you'll have to hurry. Come right back here when you're done. I'll get word to your parents that you'll be home late. And Gustave," he added, "I'm sure I don't need to tell you this, but don't say anything to anyone about what you're doing. You are a boy taking a ride on his bike, that's all."

Gustave coasted down the hill with the beret on his

head, listening to the bicycle clanking. Thoughts rushed through his head. Had Nicole made the ramp here, at the bottom of the hill? It wasn't surprising that she had broken her collarbone, riding the way she did. He hoped it didn't hurt too much. Thinking about Nicole, Gustave felt heat rising to his face. He pushed the thought away. Who was visiting the Meniers at Chenonceau today? he wondered. It wasn't anyone he knew, but soon it would be Aunt Geraldine, Jean-Paul, Giselle, Marcel, and Madame Landau, escaping from the Boches just the way Monsieur Menier's visitors were today. When Gustave was about a kilometer away from the Morins' house, he suddenly remembered that Nicole's packet of schoolwork was still at the bottom of his schoolbag, on her kitchen floor, forgotten. Oh, well. He grinned. Nicole had a good excuse for putting off doing her homework tonight!

Gustave jammed on the brakes in front of Monsieur Ferrand's café. Imagining that he was a bicyclist racing in the Tour de France, he had gotten there faster than he would have thought possible, and he was out of breath. Monsieur Ferrand's little dog, Victoire, was nosing around the legs of the outdoor café tables, looking for scraps, but the tables were all empty.

After a few minutes, Monsieur Ferrand hobbled out of the café, leaning on a walking stick. He eyed the blue beret on Gustave's head and the canvas bag in the bicycle basket.

"Nicole said to ask you how business is today—quiet or busy?" said Gustave.

"Ah," said Monsieur Ferrand. He looked at Gustave intently. "It seems quiet so far," he said. "But I have a feeling business might be picking up soon. Keep your eyes open."

Gustave nodded nervously and got back on the bike. It wobbled for a moment, then steadied. He looked back over his shoulder as he was about to turn the corner. Monsieur Ferrand had taken a seat at one of the outdoor café tables and was sitting with his chin on both of his hands, gazing meditatively out at the street. Victoire stood next to him, her outstretched tail rigid and quivering, barking at something Gustave could not see.

Business might be picking up soon? That must mean that there might be trouble. Gustave fingered the blue beret on his head. Should he keep it on even if he didn't see anything unusual? But if he kept it on, the Meniers' visitors would be delayed and wouldn't get safely into the unoccupied zone. It sounded as if Monsieur Ferrand had heard some rumors and wanted Gustave to be especially vigilant. Dusk was beginning to settle in, and it was getting cool. Gustave checked his watch nervously. Four-twenty-five. He had to check extra carefully, but he also had to hurry.

Gustave turned and bicycled down the next street and the next, glancing attentively from side to side. Nothing unusual. No one was outside. Just stone-and-stucco buildings under leafless trees. A piece of newspaper drifted down the empty street. Gustave watched as the wind picked it up, turned it over, and dropped it down onto the sidewalk, then wafted it up again. The piece of newspaper floated ahead of him, around the corner, and picking up speed Gustave made the sharp left turn around the dark corner too, following the newspaper with his eyes.

"Hey! Watch out!" Two French policemen and an older man in a black uniform suddenly loomed up out of the shadows. Gustave swerved, narrowly missing them. His bike hit a patch of gravel and skidded, crashing down onto its side on top of him. His scraped knee and elbow stung in the cold evening air. Gustave got up, brushing bits of gravel from his arms and legs. His beret had fallen off, and he picked it up with trembling fingers and jammed it back on his head.

"Are you all right, kid?" asked one of the French policemen, picking up Gustave's bike and handing it to him.

"Is *he* all right?" the man in the black uniform said harshly, in a heavy German accent. "He should watch where he's going!" Something silver gleamed on the man's cap, and when he turned, Gustave saw a red band with a black swastika on his left arm. "No discipline, you French," the man in the black uniform said, glaring at Gustave. "Where are you going, boy?"

Gustave's elbow was bleeding. "I-I'm just . . . going home," he stammered.

"Where do you live?" The black-uniformed soldier squinted at him.

Gustave's voice felt strangled, the way it had been in the dream about Marcel. But he managed to squeak the words out. "Saint-Georges."

"You'd better get on home, then," said the French policeman who had spoken before, nudging Gustave toward his bicycle.

Gustave's knees wobbled. Would the German officer call him back? He threw one leg over his bicycle and rode away, trying not to go too fast, as if he were just a boy riding home from school. The officer didn't stop him. He was speaking loudly to the French policemen. As Gustave turned the corner, he heard the German officer again bark out the word "discipline."

As soon as Gustave was out of sight, he pedaled straight toward the spot opposite the Chenonceau woods, gripping the handlebars tightly with cold fingers. Blue beret, blue beret, blue beret, he thought, in time with the rhythm of the pedals. No need to check the other streets now, of course. But what if the German officer and the French policemen followed him? He wasn't going directly to Saint-Georges, and if they followed him, they would see that. Gustave pedaled as fast as he could. The cold air burned his throat each time he gasped for breath. As he pulled up to the resting spot, his brakes screeched, and he jumped off the bike. What time was it? Four-fifty. The delay with the soldier and the policemen had made him five minutes late. Gustave left the white cap in its canvas bag in the bicycle basket and sat down, his heart hammering, on the rock where he and Nicole had sat on the day they had bicycled there together. He tried not to look toward the woods. He was very conscious of the scratchy wool of the beret on his head. What if he was too late? What if the "visitors," not seeing him, had assumed that things were safe and left the woods—and were about to get caught and turned over to the Nazis?

Gustave reached up and pulled the blue beret down more firmly over his forehead. How long should he stay there? Monsieur Morin hadn't said. Gustave pushed up his sleeve and studied his watch. He would stay ten minutes longer, he decided. But what if the Nazi soldier and the policemen came by and demanded to know what he was doing? That might give everything away. They might decide to search the woods. He had to act as if he were doing something ordinary. There had to be some reason why he would stop there, across from the Chenonceau woods, on a cold evening as it was getting dark.

The bicycle! That could be the reason. Gustave looked it over slowly, pretending that he was checking for damage. He examined the rusty old bicycle as carefully as if it had been a brand-new and shining birthday present that he was worried might have been scratched by the fall. He fiddled with the chain, ran his hands over the fenders, and used his fingers to tighten the bolts that held the seat in place. He adjusted the outer flat tire on the front wheel, straightening it over the one inside. When he had looked at everything he could think of, he glanced surreptitiously at his watch. Surely, it had been more than ten minutes by now. No, only four. He did it all over again, as slowly as he could. Six minutes.

Gustave sat down on the rock again, pulled up his sleeve, and examined his bleeding elbow as if it were a very serious wound. His sleeve was torn. Maman wouldn't be happy about that. Gustave picked at a piece of loose skin, then rummaged around in his pockets for a handkerchief and held it against the cut, looking down at it. His toes and fingers were getting numb. This was the slowest ten minutes of his life.

Suddenly, something crackled in the woods. Gustave started and looked toward the spot. No! He shouldn't look, in case someone was watching him. He quickly turned his head away, pretending to be gazing into the distance. He reached up and touched his blue beret, adjusting it on his head. He heard a rustling in the woods, but no one came out. Gustave held his breath. Still no one. No more sounds. He waited, pressing the handkerchief to his elbow, making himself count slowly to five hundred. Then he got on the bike and pedaled back toward Nicole's house as the sky grew steadily darker.

"You're here, Gustave!" Papa was just inside the doorway of the Morins' house. Papa hugged Gustave, pulling him into the kitchen. Gustave had time to notice that Nicole had found her homework and was working on it by the light of an old oil lamp before she jumped up, wincing as the movement jostled her arm, and pulled the beret off Gustave's head.

"The blue beret! Good job!" she said, swinging it around on her good hand.

Papa nodded. "I'm proud of you, Gustave."

Nicole's father was pacing up and down the kitchen.

"Well done!" he exclaimed. "Just after you left, I got word that there were Nazi officials in town, directing the French police to keep an eye on Chenonceau. They have gotten suspicious that people are crossing the line through the castle."

"I saw the police!" said Gustave. "Two French policemen and a Nazi officer in a black uniform."

"Oh, I *would* break my collarbone and miss the most exciting thing that has ever happened," moaned Nicole. "You're so lucky."

Gustave thought of the people, whoever they were, who had been waiting for his signal in the cold, dark woods, and shivered. "What will the Meniers' visitors do now?" he asked Monsieur Morin.

"I don't know," answered Nicole's father. He had stopped pacing and was leaning against the stove. "They will stay hidden in the château for a while, at least until things quiet down. Apparently, Monsieur Menier woke up in Chenonceau this morning, to the sound of axes," he went on, resuming his pacing. "The Nazis have started hacking down all the old trees on the part of the Chenonceau grounds that are on the north side of the river so that they can more easily keep an eye on the castle. The Menier family is furious about having their beautiful trees destroyed, but what can they do?"

He turned to Gustave's father. "I know that your friends and your sister-in-law and her children must already be planning their journey here, if my contacts got word to them," he told Papa, "but I'm afraid that they won't be able to cross through Chenonceau after all."

Papa's face went pale. Gustave felt as if someone had grabbed him by the throat, and he couldn't breathe.

"Do you know any other way for them to get across?" Gustave asked when he could get the words out. Nicole stepped closer to Gustave and put her warm hand in his. Gustave looked down at their two hands, clasped together for a moment. His eyes burned.

"I don't know," Monsieur Morin said slowly. "It's getting very difficult to cross the line." He looked at Papa. "And

I know your visas are good for only a little while longer. You have to get to America soon."

Papa nodded again, slowly.

"But we can't go without my aunt and cousins and without trying to help the Landaus," said Gustave hoarsely. "Can we, Papa?"

"There was a man who used to take people across the river in an illegal rowboat at night," Nicole's father said, as if he were thinking aloud. "Boats aren't allowed on the river now, of course. He sank it to the river bottom with stones to hide it under the water when he wasn't using it so that it wouldn't be confiscated. But the Nazis caught him and arrested him and his whole family two months ago."

Gustave heard Papa draw his breath in sharply.

"And in another town, there's a family with an old mill on the river Cher. They lead people across the river at night by having them walk on an old stone causeway under the water. They know where the stones are, and they help people across. But this fall," he sighed, "the water is so high, it would be up to an adult's neck, and it is so fast and so cold."

Monsieur Morin looked over at Gustave, measuring him with his eyes. "A boy about Gustave's size could swim, holding on to an adult's shoulders in case of a strong current. But with a toddler, it would be too dangerous. I just don't see how it could be done."

No one spoke for a few minutes. The old farmhouse kitchen was dark and full of shifting shadows. A cold draft slipped in through the crack of the window and blew through the room, making the light of the oil lamp flicker and rustling the pages of Nicole's notebook on the table.

"If I could just find a way to get on the good side of the guards at the demarcation line," Papa muttered. "If I just had something to bribe them with, as a last resort, I might be able to hide Geraldine and Madame Landau and the children in the back of my truck and smuggle them across. It would be dangerous, but I'm good at making friends with the soldiers if I have some little gifts to slip them as I go by. Once you get to be buddy-buddy with them, they never do a thorough search. I used to be able to get cigarettes for the guards and sometimes wine. But my sources have dried up. Do you maybe know of any way I could get some chocolate bars to bribe them with? Perhaps Menier chocolate?"

Monsieur Morin lifted and dropped his shoulders, sighing noisily through pursed lips. "I don't," he said. "The Meniers haven't had any to give away in a long time. The German trucks pull up to the factory now, and they take all the chocolate to the German army as soon as they make it. I'll try to think about other things to bribe the soldiers with. Cigarettes, wine, chocolate . . . what else do the Boches want?"

Gustave suddenly remembered a bitterly cold evening a year ago and soldiers with wide, laughing mouths and cold eyes.

"Papa," said Gustave, from the corner where he was standing with Nicole, "what about radishes? Black radishes?"

27

Monsieur Morin looked at Gustave, puzzled. "Radishes?"

A slow smile broke across Papa's face. "Radishes!" he said. "Of course! Why didn't I think of it before?" He beamed at Gustave, making him feel warm all over. "As Gustave has very good reason to know," Papa went on, smiling at Nicole and her father, "the Germans love black radishes!"

Gustave told the story, and Nicole and her father listened intently. Then Papa and Monsieur Morin worked out the details of the plan. Gustave's father would start crossing the demarcation line, working hard to get on friendly terms with the guards again. Both on this side of the line and the other side, he would use the cloth and shoes he had left to barter with, but instead of looking for farmers who had butter or cheese hidden away, he would look especially for farmers who had black radishes. He would be sure to have a few lying about to offer to the German border guards whenever he crossed over the line.

"The most easygoing soldier at the demarcation line on this stretch of the river is a redhead named Karl," said Monsieur Morin. "I'll find out when his shifts are, and you can use the radishes to get friendly with him."

"The Roberts may know who has been growing black radishes," said Papa to Gustave as they left Nicole's house. "The first time I cross, I'll stop in and see them."

Karl's next shift was on a Monday, so on Monday morning, Papa took the truck and drove off toward the line. For Gustave, it was a long day. He squirmed on his hard seat at school, thinking about his father when he was supposed to be memorizing his English vocabulary words. Was Papa at the Roberts' farm now? Did they have any radishes for him? Was he driving around the countryside? What if he stopped at the wrong farm, trying to barter for radishes, and the people weren't friendly? Even when Gustave was outside at recess, he kept wondering about Papa.

"Stop fidgeting, and study," said Maman to Gustave as he jumped up from the kitchen table for the fifth time to peer out the window. "Papa should be here a little after five o'clock our time, since he's waiting to cross at the very end of Karl's shift." But Maman fidgeted around the kitchen herself. She jumped when she heard a sound from the street outside and nicked her finger with the knife she was using to peel a potato.

"Oh, I wish he would come," she said, squeezing her thumb against her cut finger to stop the blood.

At exactly fourteen minutes after five o'clock, the door opened, and Papa came bounding into the kitchen, bringing a blast of cold, fresh outdoor air with him.

"Yes, indeed, Karl loves those radishes!" he said, thumping Gustave on the back. "I found two, and I left them on the seat next to me in a basket. He asked me—rather nicely!—if he could have one. He said they reminded him of home. I gave him both, and he was so happy, he started telling me all about his mother and the place he grew up. I chatted with him about the cloth business, and I told him I meet frequently with a client in the occupied zone. He didn't even open the back of the truck. In fact, he was one of the guards we ran into before, the day they took the radishes. The first one, the redheaded, friendlier one?"

Gustave didn't remember any of them as being friendly.

"He was on my side of the truck. Don't you remember? He laughed when I made a joke? He didn't help the other two take your radishes? Anyway, he remembered us, and he even asked where you were. Turns out he has two sons himself, one older than you and one younger. You were in school, of course, I told him."

Gustave still didn't like thinking about that day. "So, what happens next?" he asked.

"I'll go back and forth a few more times when Karl is on shift, making sure I have radishes on the return trip each time. He and I should be firm friends by the time our relatives and friends arrive at the Roberts' house, which will be in about two weeks, according to Monsieur Morin's contacts. Oh, and speaking of the Roberts," Papa went on, "they know lots of farmers in the area who might have radishes to trade, and Marguerite needs boots two sizes larger, and"—Papa pulled something out of his coat pocket—"look what I have for you, Gustave!"

"Monkey!" Gustave exclaimed. He turned Monkey over in both hands, feeling his warm fur. He wasn't much more worn than he had been last year.

"Did Marguerite cry when you took him?" he asked.

"No. I guess Madame Robert has been talking to her about giving Monkey back for a long time," Papa said. "She finally got a pass to cross the line to visit her elderly mother, who hasn't been very well. She and Marguerite have been crossing the line often, it seems, to visit the grandmother. They always brought Monkey along in case they saw one of us in Saint-Georges, but they never did. They didn't want to call attention to us by asking where we lived. It seems Marguerite has crossed the line so often holding Monkey that the guards at the line call her 'the little girl with the monkey'! The guards all think Marguerite is so cute, Madame Robert said, that they never give them any trouble."

Gustave stroked Monkey's fur and smiled at his funny little face. So, Monkey had been on this side of the line, nearby, many times, and Gustave hadn't even known. It was good to see Monkey again after a whole year, but it felt suddenly as if he had carried him around in his pocket a long time ago, when he was much younger.

Before Gustave got into bed that night, he sat Monkey down on the dresser, next to the torn picture that he still kept in the silver frame, even though it no longer had any glass in it. He looked at Jean-Paul's face and the space where Marcel's face had been. Soon, he hoped, they would be together again, all of them, the Three Musketeers. All for one—one for all. And then Gustave and Jean-Paul would leave for America, while Marcel and his mother would stay in Saint-Georges, where at least they would be safer than in Paris, with the Morins helping them. Maybe later, Marcel and his mother could get visas too and come join the others in America. Gustave couldn't imagine what it would be like living in a foreign country, learning to speak a new language. The kids there probably wore different kinds of clothes, ate different food, and played different games. How would he fit in, in a strange new place?

He climbed into bed and lay on his back, gazing up at the ceiling. America would be safe, Papa said. They were unbelievably lucky that Papa had a cousin there who could help them get immigration visas. There were no Nazis in America, no laws discriminating against Jews, no French police who obeyed the Nazis, no French collaborators— like Philippe and his grandfather—who enjoyed turning Jews over to the police.

What was it that his teacher had said that day in school, the day Gustave had found Philippe's note? Without equality and brotherhood, there is no real liberty? It was true, Gustave thought suddenly. People like Philippe and his grandfather might believe that they could be free while treating others as less than human. But their minds were trapped. Trapped by hatred. Trapped by thinking the way the Nazis told them to think.

"All men are created equal." That was what Thomas Jefferson had written long ago in America's Declaration of Independence. Gustave had learned that in school in Paris, before the war, because it had influenced the slogan of the French Republic, "Liberty, Equality, Fraternity." Everyone equal. Would America turn out to be a place that lived up to that promise?

France had not lived up to the slogan of the Republic. But France was his country, his home. Until that day in Paris a year and a half ago when he had overheard that he and his family might one day have to leave France, Gustave had not given his country or his freedom a second thought. Being French was like breathing. But when he saw graffiti saying that Jews didn't belong in France, when the Nazis marched through his country and flew their flag in France—then he knew how deep a part of him it was, being French. And how much it would hurt to leave.

Leaving France would mean leaving good people, brave people. People who weren't Jewish but who took risks to help Jews. People who believed in equality and fraternity. People whose minds were truly free. The Robert family. Monsieur Brunel, Gustave's teacher at school. Monsieur Ferrand, with his friendly little dog, at the café. Nicole's father. Nicole. Gustave thought about her laughing eyes and the feeling of her warm hand clasping his. After he and his family left for America, Gustave thought, turning onto his side and looking at the shadowy square of the blacked-out bedroom window, would he ever see any of them again?

Papa crossed the line four more times over the next two weeks. Each time, he made sure that he had a radish or two in a basket beside him on the front seat, mixed in with a bunch of rutabagas or Jerusalem artichokes, to give to Karl when he came back across the line. Then one Wednesday evening, as it was getting dark, someone knocked three quick, light taps on the door.

Gustave jumped up from the sofa, where he had been reading, and opened it. It was Nicole. She handed him a piece of folded paper, looking at him with an expression that Gustave didn't understand, then ran away into the twilight.

Papa came up behind Gustave. "From the Morins?"

Gustave handed him the note, and Papa read it. Maman stood quietly behind him in the entryway. "'Geraldine and the children ready for your help tomorrow,'" Papa read out loud. "'Unable to contact the Landaus. No further news.'"

Gustave snatched the paper and read the words over and over again, but they said exactly what Papa had read aloud.

"Why not? Why not?" he said frantically. "Where could Marcel and his mother be?" He turned to run after Nicole, but Papa grabbed his arm.

"It says 'no further news,'" he said quietly. "That's all they heard from their contact." Papa's face and Maman's were shadowy in the dark hall.

"I need to talk to you about tomorrow, Gustave," Papa

went on, moving back to the living room. "That is what we need to concentrate on now. I would like you to come with me when I go."

Maman gave a faint cry. In the lamplight, her eyes glittered with unshed tears.

"I think it will make everything seem less suspicious if you're with me," Papa continued, putting his hand on Gustave's shoulder. "It will help distract Karl to see you. He asked about you again last time I crossed the demarcation line. He misses his own sons. I told him that you were born here in France and don't speak German. He keeps telling me that we should move back to Switzerland so that you can speak German too. He was glad to hear that you were a Boy Scout. He used to take long hiking trips with his older son. He'll be even easier to chat with than he usually is if you're there with me."

"I don't like Gustave taking that risk, Berthold," said Maman.

"I know," said Papa soberly. "Do you think I would ask him if there were another way? But his being there will make everything safer all around, especially if Karl has another guard working with him tomorrow. Why would I bring my young son if I were up to anything dubious? The people the border guards tend to be most suspicious of are adults, especially men, traveling alone."

Maman nodded slowly. "We will leave the decision up to you, Gustave."

Gustave's palms tingled. "I'm coming," he said firmly.

"Good." Papa nodded. "And no questions about the Landaus until we get Aunt Geraldine and your cousins

196

safely here. One thing at a time. We all need to stay calm and focus on getting them across the line."

Papa had built a false back inside the rear of the truck, with just barely enough room for the two families squeezed tightly together. It wouldn't be so tight now. Jean-Paul and Aunt Geraldine and the baby would slip into the small space, and then Papa would pile heavy barrels and large boxes in front of it, cumbersome things that no one would want to move, especially not a soldier at the end of a long shift. A doctor who worked with Nicole's father to help people cross the line had given Papa some drops to make the baby sleep so that Giselle wouldn't cry and give away the hiding place.

But would the plan work? The plan to contact the Landaus hadn't. Where were they? Gustave bit down on his lower lip. And what if the German guards decided to examine the truck thoroughly for some reason and found the hiding place with Jean-Paul's family squeezed into it? What would happen? "Karl has never searched the back of the truck? Not even once?" Gustave asked.

"No," said Papa confidently. "He has never even opened it. And by now, he and I are well acquainted. He's a decent man, even if he is a German. He thinks of me as a friend. He'll be delighted to see you again, and, with you there, what he'll be thinking about is his sons and his home, not the black market. There's no reason at all why he would search the truck now."

28

As Gustave and Papa approached the demarcation line on their way into the occupied zone the next morning, Gustave felt his hands getting damp. But a German soldier with reddish brown curls strode toward the truck, smiling and peering in at Gustave. He and Papa immediately began to chat in German.

"Nice to see you again, Gustave," the soldier said after a while, switching into French and reaching across Papa to shake Gustave's hand. "No school today, *hein*? It is a strange school schedule you have here in France—school on Saturday but no school on Thursdays or Sundays. Do you like that schedule?"

Gustave wiped his damp palms on his pants. Of course he couldn't say anything to a German soldier about the

Jewish Sabbath. He tried to smile. "Yes, Monsieur. I like having a day off in the middle of the week," he managed.

"So school is not your favorite thing?" Karl grinned. "Just like my younger son." He nodded at Papa. "All in order—go on across."

When they were on the other side of the river, Papa and Gustave looked at each other. "You see?" Papa said. "Not a bad man. He said to me in German that you are getting tall. 'My own son will be almost a grown man when I see him next,' he said. He sounded wistful."

Gustave nodded. Karl really did seem like a decent man, one who would rather be home with his family than fighting, even though he wore a German uniform. But he was under Nazi command. And he did have a rifle. Gustave jiggled his legs nervously up and down against the front seat.

When they pulled up to the Roberts' farm, Gustave jumped out of the truck and ran toward the house. The younger Madame Robert had the door open before he and Papa got there. As soon as Gustave stepped into the Roberts' kitchen, Aunt Geraldine's arms were around him. She didn't feel as soft and cushiony as she used to, and Gustave could feel her trembling. But she still gave big, wet kisses.

"Gustave!" she exclaimed, kissing him not twice but three times, first on the left cheek, then on the right, then on the left again. "You've grown so much!" When Aunt Geraldine saw Papa, she released Gustave and swooped down on him. "Berthold!"

Gustave took a few steps back and surreptitiously rubbed

the back of his hand against his damp cheeks, embarrassed but smiling. Jean-Paul was sitting at the table, eating some bread and a bowl of soup. "Jean-Paul!" Gustave cried joyfully.

Jean-Paul looked up. He was pale and much thinner than when Gustave had last seen him, a year and a half ago. "Hey, Gustave," he said. His voice was serious-sounding and deeper than it had been before. When Jean-Paul stood up to shake hands with Papa, Gustave was surprised to see that he now came up almost to the top of Papa's ear.

It was strange to see Jean-Paul by himself when, for so long, Gustave had imagined him and Marcel coming together to Saint-Georges. Gustave's heart thudded. Couldn't he just ask Jean-Paul in a whisper what he knew about Marcel and Madame Landau? But Papa shook his head and gave Gustave a warning look. Gustave sighed and sat down next to his cousin at the table. But if he couldn't ask about Marcel, he didn't know what to say. Jean-Paul looked as if he didn't know what to say either. It seemed to Gustave as if that night he had said goodbye to Jean-Paul and Marcel in Paris had been about a hundred years ago.

Just inside the doorway, the two Madame Roberts, Papa, and Aunt Geraldine stood talking in low, intense voices. Now that Gustave looked at Aunt Geraldine from farther away, he could see that her eyes were red and that she had been crying. Papa frowned. "She has to be silent," he said. "Absolutely silent. It will cause a disaster if she cries."

Something seemed to be going wrong. Was it Giselle

they were talking about? But wouldn't the sleeping drops they were going to give her keep her quiet? "What's the matter?" Gustave whispered to Jean-Paul. "Do you know?"

"Giselle is really sick," Jean-Paul said quietly. "She has a high fever, and she keeps waking up and screaming. Maman says it isn't safe to give her the sleeping drops when she isn't breathing well."

A high, thin wail came from the floor above. Aunt Geraldine hurried up, the stairs creaking under her feet. In a few moments she came back down, nestling Giselle against her. Giselle wailed and wailed, her nose running, her dark eyes bright, her cheeks flushed. She was older and bigger, a toddler now, but it was startling to Gustave to see how thin and spindly she had grown. The last time he had seen her, she had had such funny, chubby little baby legs. Aunt Geraldine paced up and down with Giselle for a while, crooning to her, and then, when Giselle quieted, she sat down with her at the table, across from the boys. The others sat down too.

"I just don't know what is to be done," said the younger Madame Robert, rubbing her hands nervously on the back of her neck. "I'm sure Geraldine is right that the sleeping drops would be dangerous for her." Across the table, Aunt Geraldine began to weep silently, holding Giselle close.

"You have to leave soon, you say?" the older Madame Robert said to Papa.

"Yes," said Papa. His voice was thin and tight. "We have to get them across tonight or, at the very latest, tomorrow. We need to get through Spain and into Portugal, and we'll need time there to book our passage on a ship and time to make the sea voyage to the United States before the immigration visas expire."

"You could all stay overnight with us, but that just isn't enough time for the little one to get better, even if we could take her to the doctor. And bringing the doctor a strange child might arouse suspicion," said the younger Madame Robert, nervously flipping her hair away from her neck.

A small figure in a nightgown appeared in the doorway. "Baby cry," said Marguerite.

She ran to her mother and rested her head in her lap. Gustave reached out and fingered one of Marguerite's curls. Even now, when he was worrying over Marcel and about how they were all going to get back across the line, he couldn't help doing that. Marguerite's curls were still silken and light brown, just like Giselle's. The two little girls looked so similar that they might easily have been sisters, even twins.

"They look so alike, you know?" said Gustave to Marguerite's mother.

She looked over at him, her hand on Marguerite's head, as if she hadn't heard. So Gustave said it again. "Marguerite and Giselle—they look so alike."

Marguerite lifted up her head, and Madame Robert slowly looked from one child to the other. "Not to their mothers, of course," she said, smiling at Aunt Geraldine. "But to someone else, to the Germans . . . Oh! It might work! I think we have a plan!"

Marguerite's grandmother crooked her white head, looked at the two girls, and started to laugh. "Yes!" she agreed. "Of course! Giselle must wear Marguerite's red jacket. Too bad we don't have that monkey."

Gustave reached into his pocket. "But I *do* have him!" he said, putting Monkey on the table. "I brought him along to say hello to Marguerite. Here he is."

Papa and Aunt Geraldine looked bewildered. "What might work?" Papa asked.

Gustave smiled at them. "Don't you see, Papa? Giselle looks like Marguerite—and Marguerite is allowed to cross the line with her mother!"

"I will dress Giselle in Marguerite's little red jacket," Madame Robert told them, "and she'll carry Monkey, just the way Marguerite always does. Marguerite can stay here with her grandmother. I will bring Giselle with me across the line, the way I always bring Marguerite, as if we were going to see my mother. I'll cross back at another bridge so that they won't notice that I'm returning without a child."

"It's very kind of you to offer to do that," said Papa slowly. He looked from one little girl to the other. "I think it would work," he said. "They do look very alike. I've heard a lot of men say that all babies look exactly the same to them, anyway. But Giselle is so much thinner."

"So, we'll pad her with extra clothing underneath the red jacket to make her look more plump," said the older Madame Robert. "My daughter-in-law can cuddle her close, telling them the child is sick and fussy." She held her shoulders erect, her white head high, and she spoke with scornful confidence. "The Boches will never know the difference!"

29

Up ahead, in the line of waiting people, Madame Robert's bony old horse tossed his head and whinnied. Gustave could see Madame Robert, with Giselle bundled up in her arms, sitting high on the seat of her open farm cart. In the darkening sky, a fast wind drove pale clouds, covering and uncovering the rising moon. It was cold even in the protected cab of the truck. Gustave was glad that sick little Giselle had on all those extra layers of clothing.

He was more worried about Jean-Paul and Aunt Geraldine, who were wedged in the cramped hiding space in the rear of the truck. They were sure to be warm, squashed in together, but did they have enough air to breathe? Even without the Landaus, it had been a tight fit. Gustave's head throbbed. Where were Marcel and his mother? Why couldn't anyone find them? But he wasn't supposed to think about them right now.

Before they had all driven toward the line, with Madame Robert a little ahead so that they wouldn't seem to be together, Gustave had helped Papa push the heavy barrels and boxes in front of the false back of the truck. It had taken a long time to do it. A German soldier would have to be really suspicious to bother taking all that stuff out on such a cold night, Gustave thought.

Jean-Paul and Aunt Geraldine must be sitting very quietly. Once, while they were driving, Gustave heard a muffled cough coming from the back, but now that the truck was stopped in the line, the back of the truck was absolutely silent.

What if Karl's shift ended early? Gustave worried suddenly. Or what if the schedule had changed? Gustave could hear his own heart thudding in his chest, and he couldn't seem to slow his breathing. He put his hand on the basket of vegetables next to him on the front seat. It held a few rutabagas, mixed in with the plumpest, largest black radishes Papa had been able to find. Looking at them there in the basket, Gustave could almost taste them, fresh and spicy, tingling on his tongue.

The line moved forward slowly and then stopped again. Now Madame Robert's cart was at the front of the line. Behind it were two men on bicycles, followed by a farmer's truck, piled high with hay. Then came Papa's truck. The wind gusted again, tossing the branches of the trees.

A short German soldier appeared beside Madame Robert's cart. Gustave saw the reddish curls under the soldier's military cap and sighed with relief, feeling some of the tension melt out of his body. It *was* still Karl's shift, then.

But what was he doing? He had walked down the line and was speaking now to the men on bicycles. Gustave peered forward. Madame Robert was climbing carefully down from the cart, holding Giselle. The men left their bicycles in the line of vehicles and followed Madame Robert to the side of the road. Karl walked up to the farmer in the truck ahead of them, and Papa rolled down his window so that he could hear.

"Out of the vehicle," Karl's voice said loudly. "Vehicles here, people over there." He walked forward and saw Papa through the window of the truck. "Ah, good evening," he said to Papa. "New procedure. Out of the vehicle. Vehicles here, people over there." He moved on down the line.

New procedure? Gustave thought. Why? He and Papa got out of the truck, and a blast of cold wind hit them. They joined the silent group of people huddled beside the road. The fierce wind made Gustave's eyes water. He looked at Madame Robert. She had turned her body so that she was shielding Giselle from the cold blast, but Giselle wailed thinly, the wind whisking her voice away. The pointed red hood of Marguerite's little jacket was over her head, and she dangled Monkey limply from one hand. Papa bumped Gustave with his elbow, and Gustave realized what he was doing. He turned his gaze away casually, as if the woman and child ahead of him were strangers.

Karl walked briskly back to the front of the line of

vehicles and then disappeared. Gustave hunched his shoulders against the wind and buried his cold hands deep into his pockets. He looked up when he felt his father stiffen beside him. Three German soldiers wearing long coats strode toward the huddled group by the side of the road. One was Karl, and one Gustave had never seen before, but at the sight of the bulky blond one, Gustave's heart gave a great leap in his chest. It was Georg. The soldier Papa had never wanted to see again.

"Your papers," barked Georg to Madame Robert. She shifted Giselle to the other side and handed her documents to him. He examined them thoroughly, glancing at Giselle and then at the papers. "And this is your cart?" He led Madame Robert toward it and began to examine the wagon, even though it was clearly empty. He opened the wooden seat and rapped his black-gloved fist along the wood in the back.

Karl and the other soldier moved closer to stand beside Madame Robert. "Ah!" said the third soldier in French with a thick German accent. "I know this little girl in the red jacket with the monkey!"

"Yes," said Karl, smiling. "We know this little girl!"

Georg walked back toward Madame Robert. The third soldier reached out a big hand and patted the hood on Giselle's head. She wailed. "Excuse me," said Madame Robert, turning Giselle's face in toward her coat. "She's sick and fussy today."

"If she is sick, you must take her to see a doctor, Madame," said Georg smoothly, leaning in to peer more closely at Giselle. Then he said something in German to Karl, who seemed to object. Georg frowned at him and said it more loudly.

"Excuse me, Madame," Karl said to Madame Robert. "But I must examine the toy." He plucked Monkey out of Giselle's hand, and she let out a rasping wail. Gustave saw something long and sharp gleaming in Karl's other hand. He suddenly drew it back and jabbed it into Monkey's soft, round belly. Gustave gasped loudly, then snapped his mouth shut. But Georg had heard the gasp. He turned and looked toward the group of waiting people, frowning, searching their faces in the darkness. Gustave flushed, furious with himself. He was so stupid. Why did he always have to let what he was feeling show? It was just like that time he had reacted to Philippe calling him a Jew and had given himself away. He couldn't do that again. Tonight, no matter what happened, he couldn't show what he felt.

"Again," barked Georg to Karl, keeping his eyes on Gustave. Gustave felt as if Georg's eyes were boring into him. He clamped his teeth on the tip of his tongue and kept his face blank as Karl jabbed Monkey again and again, piercing his soft little body with the gleaming instrument. After a few more stabs, Karl handed the monkey back to Giselle. "There's nothing hidden inside *that* toy," he said to Georg. "No jewels, no money, nothing."

"All in order," barked Georg, sounding disappointed. "Go on."

Gustave watched as Madame Robert climbed back into the cart with Giselle on her hip. She flicked the reins. The elderly horse lifted its head and clopped slowly over the bridge, and they disappeared into the darkness on the other side. Safe! Gustave thought. Two of them, safe!

Now Karl was speaking to the two men on bicycles, examining their papers and making them open their coats. Georg and the other soldier looked at the farmer's truck, loaded high with hay.

"Is this your truck?" Georg asked the burly farmer, who was wearing a dirty, ragged overcoat. "Where are you transporting hay at this hour?"

The farmer muttered something about his brother-in-law and held out his papers. Georg examined them and said something to the other soldier, who walked back toward the truck piled high with hay. The soldier took his rifle off his shoulder and jabbed it into the hay in one spot after another. Gustave's fingers trembled, and he clenched his hands into fists in his pockets. They must be looking for people hidden under the hay. What would happen when they came to Papa's truck? Gustave felt his stomach tighten, and acid rose in his throat. He swallowed, forcing it down.

Some hay fell out of the wagon, and the farmer started forward to pick it up. "Halt!" shouted Georg. Then he barked another order in German. The soldier held his rifle up to his shoulder, gesturing to the farmer to keep back. Gustave's stomach contracted. What if someone was in there? The soldier fired between the wooden slats on the back. Then again. And again. But no one cried out, and no blood stained the hay. The farmer only muttered as more hay fell out with each rifle shot.

"In order!" Georg scowled at the farmer. "Go on! Next."

He turned to Papa. Papa's face looked gaunt in the moonlight.

"This is your truck?" he asked. "Papers."

Papa handed him the papers. Gustave noticed his father's fingers quivering slightly. But Papa answered the soldier cheerfully in German.

"From Switzerland, eh? And this is your son?" Georg barked. His eyes bored into Gustave again. Gustave's heart throbbed painfully in his chest.

"Open the back of the truck," Georg ordered Papa.

Papa walked, limping up and down, toward the rear of the truck, and the door screeched open. The soldier gestured toward the back of the truck, speaking to the other two. "Search it."

Karl and the other soldier peered in at the dark interior of the truck and the heavy boxes and bundles inside. The other soldier said something to Georg in German. It sounded like a complaint.

Georg turned to Gustave and Papa. "Too difficult to search through all that at this hour, my men say. You, boy. What do you think?" His eyes locked with Gustave's. "We have to be sure no one's hiding in there. Should we search your truck and keep you here for a few hours, or should we just shoot into the back?"

Gustave's heart hammered so hard that he was sure the soldier could hear it. But he couldn't react. If they searched, they would surely find Jean-Paul and Aunt Geraldine. And if they shot into the truck, one or both of them might be killed. But would they really want to shoot into it? Surely not. It wasn't like shooting into hay. The bullet might ricochet off the metal sides of the truck and kill the soldier. Georg was testing Gustave to see if he would act worried, and he couldn't react. He had to behave as if he were just a bored kid going home with his father.

Gustave stared steadily into Georg's eyes and shrugged. "It's too cold to stand here for hours. Just shoot, I guess. But don't hit the tires. They're impossible to replace."

Georg gave a short, sharp laugh and walked toward the open back of the truck. To Gustave, the officer seemed to be stepping in slow motion, like a person in a dream, or someone walking under water, slowly pushing his legs forward, one after the other. In an unhurried way, he lifted his rifle to his shoulder. He was really going to do it, then. It wasn't just a test. When the rifle clicked, Gustave's heart jolted.

Suddenly, Karl was at the cab of the truck, looking in the side window. He called something to Georg in rapid German. Georg lowered his rifle and strode forward to join Karl.

"Come here!" Georg barked. Papa and Gustave walked forward. Karl opened the passenger door on Gustave's side. There was the wicker basket with the rutabagas and the radishes. Georg looked in at it and then at Papa and Gustave.

They stood looking at each other in silence for a long moment, the two of them and the German officer.

"Ah!" said Georg, smoothly. "Black radishes. Very nice." He reached in and plucked the four black radishes out of the basket. He called something in German to the other soldier, who was still standing by the open back of the truck. There was a pause, and the door slammed shut.

"All in order!" barked Georg. "Go on!"

Papa and Gustave got into the front of the truck, the basket on the seat between them empty except for a few rutabagas, and Papa drove on, up over the bridge, and safely into the unoccupied zone.

30

Lisbon, January 1942

A few weeks later, Gustave stood on the deck of a ship anchored out in the harbor of Lisbon, Portugal. Leaning on the railing, with Jean-Paul beside him, Gustave watched the January sun glisten on the blue ripples of the harbor and, across the water, on the white buildings and red roofs of Lisbon. The last weeks had passed in a blur of embraces, tears, packing, goodbyes, train rides, and border crossings, first into Spain and then into Portugal, where they were to set sail for America.

The Landaus were still missing. After Jean-Paul and Aunt Geraldine had crawled, stiff and cramped, out of the hiding place in Papa's truck, after Aunt Geraldine had taken Giselle tearfully into her arms, and after Giselle had been rocked to sleep, Gustave had heard what had happened to Marcel and his mother.

"Do you remember when we last spoke by telephone?" Aunt Geraldine asked Maman. "It must have been in April or May of last year, just before the Nazis invaded. Right after we spoke, Madame Landau got a letter from her brother, who lives near Strasbourg, and she decided that she and Marcel would join him there. I didn't want her to go to Alsace—why go to the part of France nearest Germany? I asked her. But she felt safer being with her brother."

All three of the listening grown-ups gasped.

"Alsace?" Maman moaned. "Why didn't she come to us?"

Gustave couldn't understand what was wrong for a moment. Then he remembered. The Boches had taken back Alsace and Lorraine from France and made them part of Germany. "It's terrible for the Jews living there," Papa had said at the café last year, when they had looked at the map of France in the newspaper.

Something heavy seemed to be pressing down on Gustave's chest. "But what happened to the Jews in Alsace?" he whispered.

Aunt Geraldine shook her head. "I don't know for sure. But after a while, we started to hear rumors. People said that when the Germans took over Alsace, they forced the Jews out—gave them fifteen minutes to pack one bag, shoved them into buses, and then dumped them in unoccupied France, in the middle of nowhere, with no food or water. Elderly people too, and babies."

"But in the unoccupied zone?" cried Gustave. "So maybe Marcel and his mother and uncle are somewhere safe now."

"Maybe," said Aunt Geraldine slowly. "But if so, they would have written to us, or to you. And Monsieur Morin's contacts from the Resistance tried to find them, and they had no luck. After a while, we started hearing worse rumors. Some people said that other Jews from Alsace were put on trains and taken to internment camps. Camps somewhere in the south of France."

Gustave felt as if he had swallowed an enormous stone that was getting heavier and heavier every minute. The room was silent.

"Terrible things are happening now," Aunt Geraldine said after a while. "One day last summer in Paris, there was a raid in the eleventh *arrondissement*, the neighborhood right next to ours. Early one morning, the French police barricaded the streets and the Métro stations so that no one could leave. They dragged people out of bed and grabbed them on the street. They rounded up all the Jewish men and took them away. They are going after the foreign-born Jews especially, people like the Landaus. I think it is only a matter of time before they start going after us all."

Gustave looked at Jean-Paul. He was staring straight ahead of him, his eyes blank, gray. Gustave thought about Marcel making beetle spitballs and dropping the nuts down from the balcony of the synagogue. Marcel fooling around in the park, kicking a soccer ball, inventing the looking-up game. Mischievous, laughing Marcel, who had been Gustave's friend ever since they had been very young boys. Where was he now? Were Marcel and his mother in one of those terrible prison camps somewhere, living in filth, hungry and cold, maybe sick? Places where people were dying?

The Germans forced Jews onto the trains, but how could the French government keep them in prison camps just because they were Jewish?

Lying in his bed at night during those weeks after hearing Aunt Geraldine's stories, Gustave sometimes started shaking, thinking about Marcel, and couldn't stop. If the Resistance couldn't find Marcel and his mother, there was nothing anyone could do to help. How could Gustave's family go to America and leave the Landaus behind? But how could they stay in France and wait for the same thing to happen to them?

The morning after Jean-Paul's family arrived, Gustave and Papa had dug up the metal box buried by the chicken coop. Its contents were now securely stowed away. The uncut jewels were sewn under the lining of two different suitcases so that no one could steal them. And Maman had taken apart her corset to make a hiding place for the American bills, pulling out all the whale bones. Working by lamplight, Gustave, Jean-Paul, and Papa had rolled the slippery American money tightly around the delicate bones, and then Maman sewed them securely back into the corset cover. When she had finished, she also sewed Monkey back together, repairing the holes that the Germans had torn in his belly. While they were all working together, Papa had made a promise. "After the war," he had said, "I will come back to France and find the Landaus."

No one had known how to thank Madame Robert for the risk she had taken, bringing Giselle across the demarcation line.

"I know you would have done the same for me," she had

said awkwardly to Maman and Aunt Geraldine. "Mothers have to help each other. Poor little girl."

As Madame Robert was getting ready to leave, first heading for her mother's house, where she would spend the night, and then planning to cross back at a different checkpoint, Gustave slipped the repaired Monkey into her hand.

"For Marguerite," he said. "Since she doesn't have any other toys."

Madame Robert bent and kissed him. "Thank you, Gustave," she had said quietly. "I know what he means to you. Thank you."

Later, after Gustave went to bed, with Jean-Paul asleep on the floor next to him, sadness washed over him as he remembered the games that he and Jean-Paul and Marcel used to play with Monkey back when they lived in Paris. But it wasn't Monkey that he needed; it was his friends. Marguerite loved Monkey, and toys should belong to small children, who would really appreciate them. In a way, Gustave felt as if he had left Monkey behind a long time ago, in the winter last year when the line had closed, with Monkey—and Jean-Paul and Marcel—on the other side.

Saying goodbye to Nicole had been hard too. Maman had said Gustave could give her their bicycle, since it was impossible to take it to America.

"No more bumpy front tire!" said Gustave, wheeling the bicycle into the Morins' shed and propping it against the wall.

"Oh, it wasn't really that bad," said Nicole. "But I bet your mother's bicycle will go really fast. I'll see in a few weeks, when the doctor says I can use my arm again."

"You're not going to make another ramp, are you?" said Gustave.

"Maybe!" Nicole grinned, walking out with him into the road.

No one was around. Gustave reached out to shake hands. For a moment, with their hands clasped, they both hesitated. Then Nicole leaned forward, and Gustave felt her lips, warm and soft, against his face. They kissed each other quickly, once on each cheek, the way grown-ups did to say hello and goodbye. When Gustave lifted his eyes a moment later, Nicole's face was pink and her eyes were bright.

"Why do you and your father do it, anyway, since you aren't Jewish?" he asked her suddenly. "Help people escape, I mean? Work for the Resistance? It's so dangerous."

All at once Nicole's sparkling eyes were intense and serious. "For freedom," she said fiercely. "For France. Because it is the right thing to do." Then a grin broke across her face again.

"Say hello to the Statue of Liberty for me when you get to America!" she said.

Gustave saw Nicole watching from the top of the hill as he walked away. Would she and her father be all right? When would he see her again?

Giselle had recovered from her fever within a week. She turned out to be an energetic toddler who was always getting into trouble of one kind or another—chasing after the chickens next door, rubbing food into her hair, taking everything out of Maman's purse and trying to sit inside it.

She made Gustave laugh, and even Jean-Paul too, some-times.

Jean-Paul didn't laugh as much as he used to or talk as much either. But he ate ravenously whenever he had a chance. In the last two days, especially, while they had been waiting on the ship in the Lisbon harbor for the final passengers to board, Gustave had noticed Jean-Paul tearing into his meals. The abundance of food in Lisbon was astonishing after all the things they had not had in France. On the days they had spent in Lisbon before boarding the ship, Gustave and Jean-Paul had taken long walks through the street markets, gazing at the mountains of white bread in loaves of many shapes, sampling the rich, soft cheeses, eyeing the fresh fish and the brightly colored fruit. On the ship too, while they had been waiting to set sail, the meals had been good and plentiful. But Jean-Paul usually slipped part of his piece of bread into his pocket, Gustave noticed, as if he never knew when he would taste food again.

That morning, as the two families got up from break-fast, Jean-Paul had looked up as he was sliding the bread into his pocket and noticed Gustave watching him.

"You don't know what it was like in Paris," he said, blushing slightly. "Some days we had almost nothing to eat. Jews couldn't shop until late in the day, when nearly all the food had been sold. At night, Giselle would cry for hours because she was so hungry."

Gustave nodded. Of course Jean-Paul was afraid of going hungry. Thanks to Papa's skill in bargaining with the shoes and the cloth, Gustave and Maman and Papa had usually had enough of something to eat, even if it was often only potatoes or rutabaga soup. And there was more food in the country than in Paris. Jean-Paul was so thin that it almost looked as if his elbows would poke through his skin.

Now Gustave and Jean-Paul stood silently together, looking out at the light sparkling on the blue water. A few people on the deck below them were scanning the harbor. One man had binoculars. Gustave knew that he was looking for air tubes that indicated the presence of German U-boats, submarines that launched deadly attacks on ships. But the surface of the water was smooth and uninterrupted.

"Do you think my father will ever come find us in America?" Jean-Paul asked suddenly.

"Of course he'll find us," said Gustave. "After the war, when he comes home. Nicole's father promised to get him the address of Papa's cousin in America. And anyway, Papa swore that somehow he'll get back to France when the war is over. To find Marcel and Madame Landau." His voice quavered when he came to those last words. It was difficult to say their names.

But when would the end of the war come? Gustave looked out again at the serene, deep blue-green of the water, at the glimmering white buildings of Lisbon, at the cold, paler blue of the sky overhead. Looking out over all that beauty, it was hard to believe that danger could ever erupt from under the ocean or come roaring down from what had once been a peaceful sky. But it could. He knew that it could.

Gustave felt the deck begin to rumble under his feet. "We're moving!" he called out, excited in spite of everything. "The ship is leaving!"

People were beginning to gather at the railing of the deck one level down to catch a final sight of land. The upper deck, where Jean-Paul and Gustave were standing, was narrower than the lower one. The two boys looked down onto the tops of people's heads, onto men's dark hats and women's bright scarves, fluttering in the ocean breeze. Gustave caught sight of Maman's flowered skirt, and then he saw them all, his family—Maman, Papa, Aunt Geraldine, and little Giselle—squashed into a corner by the railing, looking back toward Portugal. Giselle held up a small, red-mittened hand and waved at the shore.

All of a sudden, Jean-Paul tapped Gustave on the shoulder and grinned. It wasn't quite the same grin that Gustave remembered, but it was good to see him more like his old self again.

"I know what Marcel would do if he were here!" Jean-Paul announced. He pulled the chunk of bread that he had saved from breakfast out of his pocket, looked at it for a moment, then tore it in half. He held one piece out to Gustave. Gustave took it and watched Jean-Paul crumble the bread between his hands, reach out over the railing, and scatter the pieces onto the people on the deck below. So Jean-Paul remembered that day with the hazelnuts in the synagogue too.

The crumbs fluttered down, landing on one man's hat, on another man's shoulder, drifting slowly through the air. A young woman with brown hair coiled elegantly at the nape of her neck looked up, confused.

"Snow?" they heard her say in French to her companion. "Even though it's January, it doesn't seem cold enough."

Jean-Paul laughed and looked at Gustave. Gustave smiled, tears prickling in his eyes. Jean-Paul nudged Gustave. "You do it too."

Gustave crumbled the bread in his fist and tossed it into the air. "For Marcel," he said hoarsely. The crumbs floated and drifted down, white specks against all that blue. The boys watched as the bits of bread settled softly on the unsuspecting passengers below. A gull swooped down from above, squawking, and caught a large crumb out of the air, the sunlight dazzling white on its wings.

Gustave caught Jean-Paul's eye, and despite the ache in his throat, he started to laugh.

"Snow!" said Jean-Paul, mockingly. "Anyone want to build a snowman?"

He nudged Gustave again, grinning, and started toward the staircase. Gustave took a last long look at Europe before turning to gaze the other way, over the vast emptiness of the ocean, toward America. Then he and Jean-Paul darted down the winding steps and through the excited crowd to join their family on the deck below, squinting, as they ran, against the almost painful brilliance of the morning.

Author's Note

Like Gustave in *Black Radishes*, my father was born in France in 1929. It was not an auspicious year to be born a Jewish child in Europe. Anne Frank was also born that year. But my father was one of the lucky few. He and his mother and sister escaped from France and survived the Holocaust.

Gustave and his parents follow the route taken by my father's family. They moved first from Paris to Saint-Georges-sur-Cher. They lived there for several years as the situation for Jews in France steadily worsened, before they were finally able to obtain all the right papers and begin their voyage to America. They traveled through Spain and Portugal, since both were officially neutral countries, and then set sail from Lisbon for the United States.

My father's family was fortunate in several ways that allowed them to escape and survive. Because my father, his sister, and his parents were all French-born, they were not among the first Jewish victims in France. The government of Vichy France, under Maréchal Pétain, first allowed the Nazis to take foreign-born Jews and only later handed over those who had been born in France.

Also, the village of Saint-Georges, where my father's family settled, happened to be just south of the demarcation line, so it fell into the safer unoccupied zone. At the time that my father's extended family traveled to Saint-Georges, no one knew that the Germans would occupy part of France in 1940. And certainly no one imagined the demarcation line between the two zones of France or knew where it would go. It was simply a matter of chance that their house was on the south side of the Cher, the river that divided the two zones in that part of France. In fact, just one month after my father and his mother and sister left France, in November of 1942, the Allies landed in North Africa, and the Nazis occupied the former unoccupied zone.

My father's family was also lucky because they had an American relative, an aunt in New Orleans. The United States government refused to give most European Jewish refugees permission to enter the country. Those who wanted to come to live in the United States had to obtain an affidavit from someone already living in America. This was a sworn statement promising to provide money to the new arrivals if they needed it. Most of the desperate European Jews trying to survive the war did not know anyone in the United States who could make them such a promise. My father says that conversations among adult Jews in France during the war years almost always involved the word "affidavit." "Have you got an affidavit yet?" "Can you get an affidavit?" they would ask one another. Other countries where Jews tried to find refuge also imposed difficult restrictions on immigrants. Many Jews were unable to flee to safety because of these restrictions.

During the war, the Nazis deported many Jews from France.

More than seventy-seven thousand died in Nazi camps. Approximately eleven thousand of them were children under the age of eighteen. But despite the ready cooperation of the Vichy government with the Nazis, and despite the anti-Semitism of many French citizens, Jews living in France had an unusually high survival rate compared with Jews living in other European countries. Nearly three-quarters of the Jews in France survived. This was partly because of the actions of French people like Nicole and her father in the novel, some of them in the French Resistance but many with no Resistance ties, who helped Jews hide and escape.

Black Radishes is fiction: it is not my father's story. But some events from his life are woven into the novel. Like Gustave and his family and a large part of the French population, my father's family panicked during the German invasion and took to the roads, trying, fruitlessly, to escape into Spain. Later, while my relatives were living in Saint-Georges, they were denounced to the police for supposedly signaling to British planes from the attic—but, as in *Black Radishes*, they were able to show that there was no entrance to the attic from their part of the house. Like Gustave's parents, the adults in my father's family buried their valuables in the yard behind their house and instructed the children to remember where the valuables were. They did this out of fear that the children would be left alone to fend for themselves if the parents were arrested and put in concentration camps. This did happen to Jews in the unoccupied zone, even before the Nazis occupied the area.

And one of my father's cousins had a Swiss passport. He used that passport to cross the demarcation line. Using his fluent German and his charm to befriend the German soldiers, he discovered that they loved black radishes. He smuggled food and people across the demarcation line by having black radishes on hand as a distraction.

Near Saint-Georges is the famous château of Chenonceau. The Meniers really were chocolate manufacturers who owned this beautiful, historic castle spanning the Cher. Part of the château is in what was the occupied zone and part is in what was the unoccupied zone of France. If you visit Chenonceau, you will hear the tour guides tell you about the way the château was used to help people cross from one zone to the other during World War II. And you can still buy Menier and Poulain chocolate bars in France!

While writing *Black Radishes*, I spoke with people who lived during this time, and I am deeply grateful to them for sharing their stories. I also read many memoirs and works of history. Anecdotes about people who painted dogs' tails in the forbidden colors of the French flag—blue, white, and red—appear in several places. The basic story about the boy who was forced to march and shout, "This is a German, not a Boche!" is true as well, although I imagined lots of additional details. It is also true that French people helped Jews and others cross the Cher in hidden, illegal boats. One brave family owned a mill with a stone ford under the water and helped people across by leading them over it. These events are mentioned in Robert Gildea's *Marianne in Chains: Daily Life in the Heart of France During the German Occupation*, 2003; Limore Yagil's *Chrétiens et Juifs sous Vichy, 1940–1944*, 2005; and Georgette Guéguen-Dreyfus's *Résistance Indre et vallée du Cher*, 1970. Among the many works of history I consulted, I also relied particularly on Robert O. Paxton's *Vichy France: Old Guard and New Order, 1940–1944*, 1972; Renée Poznanski's *Jews in France During World War II*, translated by Nathan Bracher, 2001; Eric Alary's *La ligne de démarcation, 1940–1944*, 2003; Hanna Diamond's *Fleeing Hitler: France 1940*, 2007; and Debórah Dwork and Robert Jan van Pelt's *Flight from the Reich: Refugee Jews, 1933–1946*, 2009.

Acknowledgments

My father, Jean-Pierre Meyer, and my aunt, Eliane Norman, shared with me many memories, sometimes funny, sometimes tragic, of their childhood in France during the war years. I am more grateful to them than I can say for telling me stories that were at times painful for them to remember. My particular thanks also go to Marie-Hélène Gold, Paul Fameau, Eliane Fameau, Irène Epstein, and Odile Donis for their memories of wartime and postwar France. Patricia Barry told me about the trees at Chenonceau, and Annette Moser, vice-consul at the consulate general of Switzerland, provided me with important details about laws regarding Swiss citizenship in the 1930s. My Wellesley colleagues, Venita Datta, Nicolas de Warren, Andrew Shennan, Vernon Shetley, Catherine Masson, Michèle Respaut, and Jens Kruse, generously shared references, books, and information about subjects as diverse as French chocolate, camouflage paint, high and low German, newsreels, Catholic traditions, and the sandbags around the monuments of Paris.

I am grateful to my agent, Erin Murphy, for encouraging me to rework the novel's opening. Susan Lubner, Patricia Bovie, Jacqueline Davies, Jacqueline Dembar Greene, Ginny Sands, and Beth Glass read drafts (and, in some instances, draft after draft) of *Black Radishes*. Their comments, advice, and encouragement were invaluable to me as I shaped the manuscript into its final form. The judges for the Society of Children's Book Writers and Illustrators' Work-in-Progress Grant, and particularly Arthur A. Levine, gave me confidence at a crucial moment through their interest in my work. A suggestion from George Nicholson about Gustave's reading material made its way into the novel. And Rebecca Short and Françoise Bui, with their patient and tireless editing, helped me to rethink crucial aspects of the book and shaped it and improved it in innumerable ways.

I am thankful to Wellesley College and to the Susan and Donald Newhouse Center for the Humanities for supporting leave time that enabled me to complete this novel. Jo Rodgers knows how deeply grateful I am to her. And, as always, I am more thankful than I can say to Ken Winkler and Hannah Meyer-Winkler for their daily love and companionship. Ken told me to put everything else aside and write this book. And Hannah reminds me every day, by her wonderful example, what actual children are really like.

About the Author

Susan Lynn Meyer was born in Baltimore and grew up hearing her father's stories about his French childhood and his family's escape from the Nazis. She studied literature and is now a professor of English at Wellesley College, where she teaches Victorian and American literature. The author lives with her husband and daughter in Sherborn, Massachusetts. *Black Radishes* is her first novel.